# TALES OF THE CAIRDS

# TALES OF THE CAIRDS

## ANNE CAMERON

HARBOUR PUBLISHING

*For Sarah Dawn,*
*David,*
*Daniel,*
*Terry*
*and Sheldon*
*with special thanks for all the hugs, kisses, smooches,*
*cuddles and snuggles*

Copyright © 1989 by Anne Cameron
All rights reserved
Published by HARBOUR PUBLISHING, P.O. Box 219,
Madeira Park, BC Canada V0N 2H0
Edited by Mary Schendlinger
Cover design by Aidan Meehan, West Coast Celtic Art
Printed and bound in Canada

CANADIAN CATALOGUING IN PUBLICATION DATA

Cameron, Anne, 1938–
Tales of the Cairds

ISBN 1-55017-004-X

1. Celts—Folklore.   2. Mythology, Celtic.
I. Title.
GR137.C34 1989   398.2'089916   C89-091386-2

# CONTENTS

In the early 1800s, there were still wandering people throughout the British Isles; story-tellers and poets, fiddlers and harpists, as nomadic as any gypsy people anywhere, and they called themselves *Cairds*. There was a similar wandering people in Norway and Sweden, and still another in Spain. Their languages were similar, their customs and beliefs similar, and they resisted for many generations the attempts of several governments to put their children in school, or to get the adults to settle in one place and become part of the society on whose fringes they preferred to stay. The Cairds owned horses, carts, caravans, and even boats; reputedly knew the magic arts; and they held gatherings once a year where they bartered, sold, and exchanged whatever surplus they had acquired during their travels. They were supposed to be able to tame any horse in minutes by whispering a secret into the horse's ear, a secret known only to Cairds and horses.

Oral tradition suggests that many Cairds were either encouraged or forced to leave the Old Countries and come to the new. Some stories even suggest they were arrested and shipped off for refusing to pay taxes, serve in the military, or stop teaching their children their own language and customs.

The Cairds themselves seem to have chosen to drop out of sight, but many of their stories remain. For generations they refused to allow anyone to write down the stories, insisting that since they refused to learn to read or write there was no way they could be sure the stories had been written down properly. Even so, the stories survived, probably changed, but all those who left the Old World changed when they came to the new. We are all profoundly influenced by our particular geography which we, in turn, influence by our building and settlement. If the stories of the Cairds have altered, they have not necessarily deteriorated.

Though the Cairds were Celtic people, their language was not entirely the same as the Gaelic spoken by the more settled people. Supposedly, a Caird from Norway could easily understand a Caird from Scotland or Spain, but the accent often puzzled others who spoke Gaelic and was considered totally incomprehensible by those who spoke English. Even so, over the years the stories were recorded, and today are remembered. Perhaps one day we will progress to the point where all differences are cherished, all cultures respected.

A.C.

The elixir of life
         of immortality
the blood red wine of Hera
Ambrosia
menstrual blood
always linked to the moon
before Avalon floated away
before Morgan disguised herself as Merlin
back
when that magic was dispensed
by the Morrigaine
her women would mark their faces
with their own moonblood
and walk proudly

# Lapis ex Caelis

*...by the power of that stone the phoenix burns to ashes but the ashes give life again...looks will not fade...appearance will stay the same as on the day she saw the stone...the same as when the best years of life began, save that the hair might turn grey...such power does the stone hold and give that flesh and blood are at once made young again.*

*The stone is also called The Grail.*
   *Stone from heaven          It fell from the heavens*

   *a stone fallen from the heavens.*

The great egg hung in the void for ages untold, and then the force of life within began to surge and pulse. The shell of the egg cracked, and through the crack came the water of life, pouring out in a torrent that became a giant river which fell from on high and touched the waiting globe. Seeds

1

were borne on the river, and from the seeds came grass and flower, tree and bush, reed and tuber, until the once barren orb was beautiful and green. Fish and birds, then, animals and bugs, all manner of creature came from the river of life, and when the world was ready, First Woman was created. Within her body she carried the seeds of life and her children were many.

When it was Time, the river of life divided itself into four rivers, and spread off in four directions. The children followed the rivers to find their own homelands, to fill the earth with the children of the Mother, to keep alive the dream and the promise, and Old Woman wove the fabric of destiny.

The ice of the earth began to spread, and the children of the Mother moved ahead of it, following rivers and streams, crossing the inland sea, moving south, ever southward, leaving behind them great carved stones so their grandchildren many-times-removed would be able to find their way back to the original homeland, and by the time the ice began to recede, these children were scattered far and wide over the earth, and still the dream of home called them.

Some of the children made their way back again, and found the inland sea was gone, in its place an ocean of grass in which grazed more animals than anyone would believe. They found valleys where the ice had not seized hold, valleys where the First Tribe had managed to survive throughout the long cold. They settled in, living together as friends, guarding the dream and protecting the promise.

Others of the children found themselves pulled by a desire they could not understand, and they searched, moving out from Persia, moving out from Libya, moving out from Africa, following the instinct they no longer recognized as the voice of the Mother. They moved through Russia and the Ukraine, and as they moved, they changed physically until they no longer resembled who they had once been.

Banba left the encampment and went to the thicket by the stream which drained from the small sweet-water pool. She sat smoothing the sand, removing the pebbles and the rocks, preparing the place and making it as comfortable as she could, then she lay curled on her side, hugging her knees, her swollen belly heaving with contractions.

The infant girl came easily, but the afterbirth refused to follow. Time and again, Banba's body convulsed in vain, then the placenta ruptured under the pressure and blood seeped from her body, soaking into the dry desert earth beneath her. She held her daughter and spoke softly to her, believing her drowsiness was natural after the effort of labour and birth. The newborn nuzzled close, her eyelids fluttering, one fist jammed into her mouth.

When the brilliant light flashed across the heavens the young mother, Banba, little more than a girl herself, was almost dead, her body exsanguinating, her mind drifting. She had no idea what the light was or what it meant, and it was only coincidence that out of all the seconds of eternity, her fluttering eyelids were open at precisely that pinpoint in the ocean of time, only coincidence that her dying eyes focused, however briefly, on the light.

Although there are many people, most of them clever, who deny the existence of that which is referred to as coincidence.

The light flared against the purple-black of the velvet night sky, and Banba's body trembled, each and every fibre of her being altered, made different, made more than merely human, made both ordinary and extraordinary, become what we all are, but something else, too.

The stone fell to earth, flaming with something hotter than mere fire, consumed as it plummeted, so that what might have been a mountain when it was first catapulted into the heavens was but the size of a small hen's egg when it came to rest in the sand beside the child-mother.

Banba's chest heaved, her lungs expanded, she took the deepest and most important breath of her life, and the air she drew into her lungs was scented with the perfume of lilies and roses, mayflower and apple blossoms. The torn placenta slipped from her body, the haemorrhaging stopped, the cells of her body stopped deteriorating and the encroaching chill faded. She slept briefly then, her skin pallid and clammy, her mind floating in some land she had never seen. The infant, lying on her mother's body, stirred and wiggled closer, seeking warmth, comfort, nourishment.

It was the child's wail awakened Banba. She rolled onto her side and moved the infant so she could suckle. Then, looking past the child's small head, Banba saw the stone. It was blue streaked with green, it was pink streaked with black, it lay in the sand gleaming, still hot, pulsing white and blue, giving warmth, giving life, giving comfort, giving strength. Banba reached out with one hand but did not touch the hissing stone. She closed her eyes, not really sleeping, not entirely awake.

The infant nuzzled, her mouth closing demandingly on the nipple, and sucked strongly. Banba's body was practically desiccated. There was barely enough fluid left to keep her heart pumping, but something— something—pulsed from the stone, along her outstretched fingers, through her hand, along her arm. The child drank, then slept.

The sky was light and the first sounds were celebrating the day, the song of birds, the bleating of sheep and goats. Banba saw the hide tents of the nomadic people but she could not remember what they were. She saw animals but was ignorant of their use, she saw people moving toward her but had no reason to know they were her husband and two of her sisters. Nothing meant anything to her, nothing had reason or importance to her. She was actually younger than her own newborn daughter, for the child had been hours old when the stone fell from heaven and gave Banba rebirth.

The young husband and the two sisters saw Banba lying in a wide dark stain of blood-soaked sand. They did not see the stone, they did not smell the fragrance, they did not think the pulsing lights and colours were anything more than the false-water mirages they had learned to ignore. What they did see was the wide-open unblinking eyes, the sand stained black with blood, the child lying without moving. They were so used to death, so used to infant mortality, so conditioned to equating blood with fatality, that they believed immediately the evidence of their own eyes.

They wailed and screamed, they grieved and mourned, they rolled on the sand and howled. Banba tried to speak to them, not because she wanted to comfort them, not because she recognized them, but only to try to stop the dreadful noise. She made a sound deep in her throat, she even managed to lift her hand, but the three who had once loved her misinterpreted and thought the dead body had been taken over by a daemon. They shrieked in terror, whirled, and fled, stumbling and screeching. Banba did not care if they left or stayed as long as the terrible noise stopped. She sighed, closed her eyes, and slept.

It was the uproar of the hysterical trio moved the

5

young black bitch from the nest she had made and in which she had given birth to her first litter of puppies. The screaming and hollering, the wailing and roaring reminded her that her bladder was distended, her bowels rumbling. She stood, nuzzled her puppies, sniffed them, pushed them closer together to keep each other warm, then she moved away from the noisy encampment to stretch her cramped muscles and relieve herself.

The nomadic people needed only to hear that Banba had died and her body been taken over by a daemon, and they were racing in panic, stuffing their few possessions in carry-packs, hauling down their skimpy hide tents, gathering up their waterskins and cooking pots. The black bitch had not yet reached the camp when the hysterical people chased their herds of tough goats and stringy sheep away from the cursed place. She raced faster than she had ever moved in her life, but she did not get back in time to divert the herds or die with her helpless puppies. By the time she got there, they had been so trampled into the dirt there wasn't even a damp spot.

The young bitch lay grieving, glaring at the cloud of dust left in the path of the ones who had caused this to happen. She nursed her pain and her grief, madness threatening to engulf her spirit.

Banba wakened, blinked her eyes, and saw at once that the stone was cool, the tents and animals gone, the shadows lengthening as the hot desert sun moved toward the distant horizon. She reached for the stone and curled her fingers around it, and in that split second she knew what she needed to know. She knew that the child suckling was her daughter, she knew her daughter had come from her very own body, she knew how the child had come to grow inside her. She even knew her own name, Banba. She did not know from whose body she herself had come. She supposed, forever after, that she was the child of the stone that had fallen from the heavens, and since her own child was suckling and nuzzling at her body, Banba picked up the stone and put it to her mouth, her lips pressed against it, her tongue licking it, her entire body throbbing and pulsing with something stronger than life itself.

She did not sleep. She sucked on the stone until her daughter's belly was full, then Banba rose and began to walk to the stream. She did not wonder how she knew there was water there, or how she knew she needed to drink, she accepted that she knew, accepted even that she knew water was precious, and vital.

She knelt by the stream, bent forward, put her face in the water and drank deeply. When she lifted her face she realized, with no feeling of shock at all, that her hair was white, the whitest white she had ever seen. She smiled and the reflection in the pool smiled back at her.

Banba put her daughter Macha in the pool, and washed the dried blood from the infant's body. The baby squirmed protest, opened her mouth, and wailed with fury, flailing her tiny hands and feet. Banba's smile turned to laughter, and she was filled with love for this wonder which had come from her own body. When the child was clean, Banba wrapped her in the cloth she usually wore over her head and shoulders, then put the child on the ground and stepped into the water herself, washing her own body and the stained tunic that hung from her shoulders to just below her knees.

She came from the pool cleansed and refreshed, the wondrous stone clutched in her hand, an egg-sized sweet-scented marvel she knew the rest of the world would kill to get. The stone pulsed and Banba's body responded; her hand lifted the stone to her mouth, her mouth opened, she swallowed. If it had been any ordinary stone or if she had tried to swallow it before the magic had changed her forever, Banba would have choked to death, but now the perfumed stone slid easily down her throat and settled comfortably in her stomach. Banba picked up Macha and headed off across the desert, her steps firm and bold.

She walked all night, holding her daughter tenderly, feeling stronger with each passing minute, nourished by the lapis ex caelis in her belly. During the night the stone taught her to take the cloth she had once worn over her shoulders and head and fashion a sling to hold Macha safely and comfortably, leaving Banba's arms and hands free. The stone taught her other things, many other things, and by the time the sun leaped from its place of rest, Banba knew more than she had known before she was reborn. And all night as she walked, she knew she was being followed by a grief-crazed bitch who was waiting for a chance to do to Macha what the terrified idiots had done to her puppies.

In the morning the dog moved forward, hate burning, eyes glaring, but then the scent of the stone came to her on Banba's breath. Scent of lily, scent of roses, scent of cinnamon, scent of something without name on this earth, and the dog moved forward, heart healed, brain strong, tail wagging. "Chu," said Banba, and it was Chu who leaned against the woman's leg, it was Chu who thrilled to have her head scratched. "Good Chu," Banba crooned.

That night they slept together, the woman, the infant, and the dog, and only they knew whether it was Banba or Chu provided the milk the child Macha suckled.

When they wakened, the child was sitting upright,

playing with her own toes, laughing and happy. Banba knew no ordinary newborn could sit so strongly or laugh so loudly; she also knew no ordinary newborn would have grown so much hair overnight, and every bit of it as white as her own.

Banba was thirsty and so was the bitch Chu, so Banba stamped her foot and the earth spewed water for them. When they had drunk their fill the water returned to the earth, leaving several large fish flopping in the sand. Banba gathered dry sticks, knocked them together, and there was a fire. She cooked the fish, sharing them with Chu, and then they moved on again, woman, child, and dog. And when next they stopped to rest the child had teeth, and could eat the same food as the woman and the dog.

They moved on, staying away from the nomadic people, staying away from those who thought Banba evil, staying away from those who had caused the death of Chu's babies and might well cause the death of her own dear daughter, and who knows how long they lived like that? And does it even matter? They walked and they fished, they gathered berries and wild food, they saw everything there was to see, and in the seeing, they learned.

At some point, it doesn't matter when, Chu began to whine, then to bark.

"Show me," Banba urged, and the dog moved forward.

"Wait here," Banba said, but her daughter shook her head stubbornly.

The trap had been set in a tree above the animals' path to the water, and the mare was caught in it, trapped so that she could barely move. Banba knew the horse was destined to be supper if the hunters found it.

"Hush," she said, but the horse still struggled. "You have to be still," she said, "or we won't get you out and

9

the next ones to come will kill you." But still the horse struggled.

Then Banba's daughter was pushing past her, moving unafraid to the horse's head, patting the animal and whispering to it. The mare stopped her thrashing, bent her head as the child leaned forward to speak in her ear, and was calmed.

They had only their fingers and teeth, their wits and their determination, but they got the mare free of the net, and led her to where she could drink safely.

"If the hunters have set their traps here we mustn't stay," Macha said firmly.

"The child gives advice to the mother," Banba teased.

"I," the little girl replied confidently, "am older than you are, you told me yourself!"

"I should have told you nothing," her mother answered. "I should have left you in the dirt and gone off by myself." But neither of them believed her words.

Banba patted the animal and then suddenly she was up on the mare's back and the world was changed forever. Her child stared up at her and Banba laughed softly, then reached down her hand. "Come," she invited, "sit in front of me." Macha reached up her own hand, Banba took it, and as easily as that, they were both riding away from the place of danger, Chu loping alongside.

"What was it you whispered to the horse?" Banba asked.

"A secret," the girl teased, "and if I told you, it wouldn't be a secret any more."

"Listen to this," Banba marvelled, "the one who almost caused my death is talking to me in such a manner," and they laughed softly, knowing it was not the birth of the child had nearly caused Banba's death, for the child had slid easily into the world. Macha pulled gently at Banba's white hair, Banba lowered her head, and her daughter whispered to her the secret she had whispered to the horse.

"Oh," Banba marvelled, "how wonderful!"

Together they moved through the days and nights of their lives, Banba, her daughter Macha, the mare, and the bitch. The dog taught them there was food to be found in the nests of birds and in the bodies of small animals, the horse made travel easier than it had ever been, and the woman learned from the girl who learned from the woman, and life was more than merely tolerable.

Sometimes they found sheep or goats that had strayed from the herds of the nomadic people, and sometimes the animals were not strays at all, but taken at night by stealth. Sometimes they needed clothing, so they went at night and stole it. Sometimes it was a knife they took, or a bowl, or a warm cloak, or a blanket. Remembering how the wandering people had deserted them, cursed them, left them to die, they took what they needed when they needed it.

The tribesmen had no idea who it was would come in silence and make off with sheep or goats or other things. They had long ago forgotten the woman and child they had left to die. They invented wild tales of magic and mystery, and they spoke of beasts that could attack and devour an entire herd, then change form and move unsuspected as a man among men. They talked of giants and dwarfs, of phantoms and shades, and they scared each other half silly with each retelling of old lies.

Sometimes, and only when the free ones wanted, the tribespeople would see Banba and her daughter riding the horse. Instead of taking it as a lesson and learning to ride themselves, they spoke of an animal part human, part beast—and the human half two-headed at that. They told each other if ever they could find where

11

this magical creature lived they would never need work again, or fight again, or do without again, for, they convinced each other, enormous treasure awaited the one who found the lair of this dreaded beast.

Banba and Macha did not know the people were inventing stories about them. They heard scraps and bits of the stories at night when they crept unseen close to the campfires of the nomads, but they never dreamed the fierce people were talking about them. They believed there really was a land of marvel, believed the tribespeople knew where the hybrid creature lived and were going there. They believed they were following the tribespeople when in fact the nomads were trying to follow Banba and Macha. In this way, they moved over land and over sea, over desert and over mountain, and though generation after generation of humans was born, lived, and died, Banba and Macha did not significantly change. The story of the damned woman and cursed infant did change, evolving gradually into the story of the blessed woman and holy daughter, and each version was as true as the version that came later and was even more changed.

One day Banba looked at her daughter and realized that the young woman not only looked as old as Banba did, she actually looked just a bit older.

"When I was younger than you," she remembered, "I was married and had a child."

"Yes," said her daughter. "Yes, and you were not lonely."

"Are you lonely?"

"Yes," Macha admitted, "I have watched other people dance, and listened to other people sing, and observed their lives for so long now, and in all that time the only person I have talked with is you."

"Well, then," Banba sighed, "I suppose we must do something about it."

Banba and Macha moved steadily toward the settlements of the herding people, living nearer and nearer to them. Bit by bit the people of the tribes grew to know the women, and began even to think of them as part of their own. When they no longer glared suspiciously at the two women, Banba moved closer, then even closer and soon she and her daughter were living among the travelling people, and Macha had all the company and all the friends she could want.

The truth of it was, Jehovah God was angry. More than just angry, Jehovah God was in a full-scale tooth-grinding hair-tearing rage.

First off, there was the matter of His Holy Name, Yhwh or Jhwh. Someone, somehow, somewhere along the line had lost the vowels, leaving only consonants, and the human tongue just isn't fashioned to talk nothing but consonants. Without the precious vowels, sound becomes noise and language becomes jargon, with nothing communicated and less understood. In the beginning was the word, but if the word is unpronounceable, people tend not to pay much attention to it. Lip service cannot be paid if the lips cannot twist themselves around the words.

Human lips could, however, twist easily around the many-vowelled Baalat, and were doing it with increasing frequency, even extending the name and the joy they took in saying it, extending it to Belit, Belit-ili, even to Beltis and Bilitis. They went to the temple and, ignoring Yhwh, they prayed to Baalat, sang to her, and took offerings to her. Calves, mostly, and Jhwh was very touchy around calves, cows, and even goats — unless, of course, they were sacrificed to him. Unfortunately, if your name is unpronounceable, people aren't inclined to direct prayers in your direction, and if they aren't calling on you to fulfill their desires, they don't have any reason to want to get on your good side, so the number of golden calves, burnished ewes, and silver-horned goats sent Yhwh's way was small and getting smaller.

And the people were living riotous lives, having parties in the name of Baalat, having other parties in the name of Belit-ili and Bilitis and Ashtarte, having parties in the name of and to the glory of Epona the mare-headed goddess, but who was celebrating in the name of a name nobody could pronounce?

Noah.

Of all of them, only Noah was worshipping and honouring Jhwh or Yhwh, and Noah wasn't one for giving or having fun parties. Oh, he observed the observances and prayed the prayers, he disciplined his sons and let not his heart refrain from their grieving, he dutifully and with grim piety did what Yhwh told him to do, but not for Noah the loaf of bread, jug of wine, and happy song on the lips. Still, humourless or not, imaginative or not, fun or not, he was obedient and if you can't have love and affection, obedience will do.

Yhwh announced his coming. He rolled the thunder and cast the lightning bolts, he caused the winds to howl and the seas to churn. Instead of cowering and trembling, instead of repenting and smartening up, the people shrugged and said, "Oh, it's that guy with the weird name having another tantrum." They continued to honour the mother figures who, of course, put their warm and loving hands over the heads of the people and kept the worst of Jhwh's wrath from coming down on them.

Noah, however, looked at the signs and portents and knew something was about to happen. And it did. Jhwh descended from on high and showed himself to Noah and said unto him, "I'm going to wash this riff-raff off the face of the earth. I'm going to cause it to rain as it hasn't rained since I don't know when, and the waters will rise until the entire earth is covered, then the waters will rise some more, and one way or the other, sooner or later, at whatever cost to whomever, things around here are going to change and be the way I want them to be."

"As Thou sayest, oh Lord God Most High," Noah answered.

"Build yourself an ark," Himself commanded, "and here are the measurements."

Noah took the blueprint in his hands and stared, uncomprehending. Yhwh reached out, turned the blueprint right side up, sighed, and mustered what little patience he possessed.

"When this boat is built," he said, slowly enough for even Noah to understand, "you will fill it with animals. Two of every kind of animal. One male animal and one female animal." He tried to cover all the bases because Noah was not what anyone would have called a quick-witted patriarch.

"And," Yhwh said sternly, "the only people who are to go in are you, your wife, your sons, and your sons' wives. All others, regardless of anything they might say, are doomed and damned. Understand?"

"As Thou sayest, oh Lord God Most High," Noah repeated.

"Noah, his wife, his sons, his sons' wives. Nobody else. Is that clear?"

It was clear. And as soon as Yhwh went back to that place from whence he had come, Noah set about having the ark built.

You can imagine the size of the thing. Never mind the cubits high or the cubits wide, pay no attention to the cubits long or the cubits deep, think of the load the thing was supposed to take. Think of the animals. Elephants and giraffes, rhinoceros and zebra, horses and cows, dogs and cats, jaguars and tigers, lions, buffalo, elk and moose, bears and raccoons, marmots and kangaroos, the list goes on and on and on; and Noah had been told to take two of each kind. How huge a space would you need for two grey whales? How much room do you need for a pair of musk ox? Camels and pigs, llamas and donkeys, chickens, turkeys, geese, ducks, cougars, wolves, and each of them needing food, each of them needing space, each of them needing shovelled out and cleaned up, each of them needing water to drink and air to breathe. Noah could have thrown up his hands and said it was impossible, but he didn't have the imagination for that. Jhwh had told him to do something, and Noah would do it. Helped by his wife, his sons, and his sons' wives.

Messengers went out with order forms, so many timbers of such-and-such a length, so many girders, so many thisses and so many thatses. Struts and ribs and crosspieces and mangers and stalls and shovel handles. Armies of workers were issued hundreds of thousands of axes and sent out to hack down entire forests. Hordes of haulers and pullers, scads of lifters and toters, phalanxes of bookkeepers and auditors, legions of assistants and apprentices.

"Crazy old coot," said some.

"Won't he look a fool," said others.

"Where's he getting the money?" asked many.

"What if he's right?" asked a young woman.

"Oh, Cessair," they laughed, "you've got to stop asking questions like that! There is no way at all he can be right! Flood the earth? Be reasonable."

"What if he's right?" Cessair repeated.

"It isn't possible to flood the earth. How could it possibly rain so much?"

"Why not?" she asked, but everybody laughed at her, and she walked off, sulky, angry, and more than ever convinced there were others besides Noah and his family who were short some of the basic necessities.

"I don't think he's crazy as a coot," she muttered. "A crazy coot couldn't get himself so organized in his fixation. He knows exactly how many nails he's going to need. He knows exactly how many hammers will wear out pounding all those nails. I think maybe he's on to something."

"Oh, I'm sure he is," Banba agreed quietly. "After all, Noah said Yhwh was in a foul mood, and sure enough, he shows up in a cloud of lightning, filling the air with the scent of brimstone."

"You don't think Noah is crazy?" Cessair asked.

"I don't think YOU are crazy," Banba corrected. "I've never been sure of Noah's mental stability. The man can't even throw a decent party!"

"What are you going to do if it rains?" Cessair asked.

"Me?" Banba shrugged. "Oh, I think I'll be ready for it." She waved casually in the direction of the docks where the Phoenician traders were arriving by ship at increasingly frequent intervals. "There are a lot of boats down there and sooner or later one of them ought to come up for sale."

"Boat?" Cessair frowned. "You mean...ride 'er out?"

"He said," Banba lectured, "that it was going to RAIN. He didn't say it was going to blow a hurricane, or storm for ten years. Rain. Drizzle drizzle drizzle."

"Float 'er out," Cessair agreed.

"That's it," Banba smiled. "Me, my daughter, my dog, our horses, maybe a canary or two just in case dim-bulb down there overlooks them...and, of course, my daughter's kids."

"Would you like some company?" Cessair asked. "Some help with all the kids, perhaps?"

"That would be lovely," Banba agreed.

They went to the docks and spoke with the Phoenicians, they listened to the talk and hearkened the gossip, then Banba went into the hills with only her dog and her horse. She told a bit of a lie at that point: she told her daughter and Cessair and all the kids that she was going to pray, but that wasn't what she did at all. She went beyond the walls of the town, past the fields and meadows, into the rugged regions of the country, and sat with one hand on her belly, over the place where the heavenly stone was still lodged, and she thought about ships, and price, and how to pay. Then, when the stone knew what it was she needed, Banba stood up, stamped her foot as she had once stamped for water, and the earth split open for her.

She returned to the docks and before much time had passed she was the owner of not one but three fine tall ships. The Phoenicians smiled at each other and talked contentedly of fair exchange being no robbery, all of them dreaming sweet dreams of how they would enjoy the wealth of jewels Banba had paid for the boats. It beat the hell out of shipping mountains of timbers for that old fool's animal craft, said one.

Over at Noah's place the work was proceeding apace. Day after day, from dawn to dark, the hammering went unabated. Measuring and remeasuring, fashioning and shaping, taking possession of material and using it so more had to be ordered and shipped. Wagonloads of material were brought and off-loaded, the wagons returning empty to be refilled and another load of material brought. Saw saw, plane plane, sand sand, nail nail, hammer hammer, until the neighbours were ready to go right out of their gourds with the seemingly endless noise and uproar.

With all the coming and going, to-ing and fro-ing happening over where Noah toiled, nobody noticed at first that Banba and Cessair were gathering supplies and preparing for their own little project.

"Hey, Noah," shouted Bith, "if you're right and Jhwh sends the flood and the world is submerged. . . what about me?"

"It is not permitted that you enter my ark," Noah said firmly. "The enormity of your sins is such that you too will be submerged."

Bith thought that was funny, and so did Fintan and Ladra, but their laughter weakened as the work progressed. Their eyes began to shift uneasily, and then Bith noticed that his daughter Cessair was spending a lot of time with old Banba the outlander and her daughter, who was mother of all those children.

"Hey, what are you doing?" he called. "And why aren't you at home getting my supper ready for me?"

"I have my work cut out for me right here," Cessair said firmly. "You might be willing to just stand around and drown, but some of us plan to help ourselves."

"Oh yeah?" laughed Fintan. "You and who else?"

So Cessair named the women who had joined Banba and her, and they were fifty of the most adventurous, fifty of the bravest, fifty of the most intelligent, fifty of the strongest, healthiest women on the face of the earth.

"Well," Fintan flirted, "why not let me help? I've done a bit of navigating in my time and I'm sure I'd be good company."

Banba laughed to herself, but made no objections, and the three men made arrangements to join the women.

"The one condition," Cessair said firmly, "is that from now until forever, I am the head of this expedition."

"Why you?" asked Ladra.

"Because Banba said she didn't want to be bothered and her daughter has her hands full with all those kids," Cessair answered easily.

"Don't be foolish!" Bith exploded. "I am your father! I am not going to take orders from you."

"Fine," Cessair shrugged, "off-load yourself and find some other way to survive the flood."

"Oh yeah?" Bith challenged. "And what if I just find some nice quick way to off-load YOU?"

"Oh, I don't think so," Banba said quietly. "After all, I am the owner of these boats, and if you try to off-load her, you'll have me to deal with. Try to off-load me and my dog will rip out your throat, try to touch the dog and the horse will trample you, look sideways at the horse and my daughter and her children will be all over you like hives."

"Oh," Bith nodded, as if convinced of something logical. "Oh. Well, right, then. For the time we're on the boat, you're the boss. After we get off the boat—"

"Right," Cessair laughed, "after we get off the boat you can piss off!"

Noah was still working on the very beginning of the skeleton of his ark and hadn't even started the monumental task of collecting animals, but Cessair, Banba, and the rest weren't of a mind to just sit around getting fat and watching him hammer, nor were they interested in waiting and letting Jhwh make the first move. They had food, they had fresh water, they had everything they needed thanks to the glittering jewels the earth had offered when she split herself open for Banba. They had, in short, everything a woman could want, and so on a Tuesday, the fifteenth of the moon, the little fleet sailed from the Isles of Meroe to the Nile in Egypt. In Egypt they were joined by Egyptus, a woman of the ruling house, and by Scota, who was the daughter of a wealthy family.

20

They were ten years in Egypt, touring and visiting, oohing and aahing, seeing wonders and marvels of which they had previously only heard. Then they sailed for twenty days to reach the Caspian Sea and twelve days on the sea itself to reach the Cimmerian Sea. One day from Asia Minor to the Torrian Sea, then a sailing of twenty days to the Alpine mountains. From the Alps it was nine days to Spain and another nine days from Spain to Dun Na mBarc, and in Corco Duibne they took the harbour on the fifth unit of the moon, a Saturday.

Two of the ships were wrecked on the rocks, but the women were saved for they could all swim. They salvaged what they could from the wrecked ships and they reached the rocky shore with all their goods and necessities. Banba was especially careful to moor the surviving boat safely for, as she told her daughter, a woman never knows what the future holds.

The men, however, had been deprived for many years of what they considered to be an absolute necessity. They clamoured amongst themselves, flirting competitively, arguing in jealousy, so Banba went to Cessair and whispered to her, and Cessair laughed heartily and whispered to the other women. Then, with all the women laughing, the division took place.

Cessair and sixteen other women took Fintan, Barrfhind and sixteen other women took Bith, Banba and fifteen other women took Ladra, who complained bitterly that he had less than the other two men.

"Oh, shut up!" Banba laughed. "Most men would consider themselves lucky to have one woman and you've got sixteen!"

"But they have SEVENteen each!" Ladra screeched. "It isn't fair!"

"We'll work overtime," Banba promised, and she must have kept her promise for within a very short time, Ladra was dead of an excess of women and was the first man to be buried in the new country.

The women who had granted Ladra's wishes went back to Cessair and told her that he who had complained he didn't have enough women had actually died of having too many, and when they had all finally quit laughing they contacted the women who had taken Bith and told them the great joke, too. The women re-divided themselves. Twenty-five of them took Bith and twenty-five took Fintan, and the others decided not to bother with the men at all for some were already pregnant and others were not interested in either of the two men who remained.

Fintan, who had always considered himself a great lover and a charming flirt, found twenty-five women more than he could even begin to imagine himself handling and he escaped, fleeing across Ben Suainme, across the Suir, over Sluib Cua in the headland of Febra, to the Shannon eastward, to Tul Tuinda over Loch Dergdeirc. Bith, the father of Cessair and not a young man before the beginning of the voyage, was soon dead himself. Only Fintan was left hiding in the hills, terrified of the women, who sometimes saw him half-naked with his hair hanging to his shoulders, his eyes so wide the whites showed, his mouth moving constantly as he recited the names of the women and trembled with the knowledge of his own limitations.

The flood predicted by Noah finally arrived and the women were ready for it. They had salvaged planks and beams from the wrecked ships and gathered fallen trees that had washed onto the beaches. They made a raft big enough to hold them and their herds and, in the middle of the raft, built a house where they could stay warm and dry. The animals lived on the deck of the raft and the falling rain washed away what a host of people with a ton of shovels would have taken most of the day to pitch over the side.

Fintan, of course, refused to get onto the raft with all those women. He detested the idea of drowning and didn't think much of the idea of getting wet, so he changed himself into an eagle and flew from crag to crag, hiding in caves, squalling to himself and nagging ceaselessly. To this day you can often see Fintan sitting hunched in a tree mumbling to himself and from time to time giving vent to a queer, wavering cry.

When the water finally began to recede, the women debarked from the huge raft and went into the hills and beyond the hills into the fertile valleys, to plant crops from the seeds they had saved, and to live life the way they wanted to live it, with singing and dancing, with laughing and loving.

The learned men of the Chronicles would have us believe the women were trapped when the waters of the flood covered the face of the earth, and it may be that they would have us believe it because then we would not wonder what happened when the next wave of takers arrived from Greece. They were led by Partholon, who was followed by the Fir Bolg and Fir Failian, then the Tuatha De Danaan and the sons of Mil from Spain. The learned men tell us that each of these takings was pure and without women, but the men who came with each successive taking spoke of Macha, the queen of the phantoms, spoke of Macha Alla the Mother of Life, spoke of the Morrigaine who haunted the battlefields, spoke of the faery queen Mab and of Erinya the mother of Eirenn itself, so obviously there were women there when the takers arrived to take.

Women who sighted the first ships knew to stay out of their way, to slip quietly from their presence, until the men began to talk of magical women who could appear and disappear at will, women who could vanish into the very earth, women who could do magic which

23

would make any man forget whatever it was the women wanted him to forget. In time the men spoke of a magical land where time had no meaning. Those fortunate enough to chance upon it would be fed delicious food, given wondrous wine, and pampered in every possible way by the most beautiful of women, each of them enchanting and proud.

Banba, however, was not among them. After the flood and before the first takers, she got busy cleaning and preparing the last of the three boats she had obtained from the Phoenicians.

"But why?" Macha asked repeatedly. "This is a lovely green land, there is music all day long and laughter half the night."

"You have what you wanted," Banba told her daughter, "but this is not what I seek. You were lonely, and now you have company, you felt alone and now you have family, but the soles of my feet itch and my eyes turn always to the horizon. Some of us are born to settle and some of us are born to travel."

"But you're my mother!" Macha protested.

"For as long as you live," Banba agreed, "and more to the point, for as long as I live. That does not mean," she smiled, "that we must live in each other's pockets. You have children, you will have grandchildren, great-grandchildren, and you wish to stay. I have no wish to stay, so I'm off to see what I can see."

There was, if you remember, one of the Phoenician boats which had not been destroyed when the women arrived in the harbour. It was this Banba took for her journey. The boat ordinarily required two or three dozen men to keep the sails in place, the decks clean, and the repairs done, but Banba had no trouble doing it alone. This should surprise nobody—there are scores of other examples in the lifetimes of each of us would provide similar examples.

Banba travelled on the ship for years, stopping regularly for fresh water, food, and whatever else she required, and feasting her eyes on everything she saw. She bought cargo in one place, delivered it to another, she took freight from here and transported it to there, she accepted passengers in one place and took them safely to another.

There was the tribe of Sarah, people who had lived following the rules and the religion of their great-grandmother, minding their business, keeping their customs, growing up, falling in love, getting married, having children who grew up to mind their business and repeat the cycle.

But forces were at work, and laws were passed, and soon the children of the tribe of Sarah were not allowed to move freely, for no other reason than that they called themselves the children of Sarah. So they changed their name to the children of Dan and they were allowed to move as they had always moved, following their flocks and minding their business.

But there were those who for reasons of their own turned things upside down and inside out, who brought in more rules and enforced them with weapons of war and hearts hardened to stone. The children of Dan, who had once been the children of Sarah, were denied the right to marry within their own tribe. Girls raised by the ancient customs were married to men who had been raised scorning the soft and honouring the stern, and year by year there were fewer and fewer of the children of Dan, who had been the children of Sarah. Other enforcers passed other laws, and more laws, until merely moving from one place to another with any of the children of Dan became in itself a criminal act.

Three times did the followers of the grim and stern one pass laws evicting the children of Dan from the land many now called the holy land, or the land of righteousness. The children of Dan were expelled once for continuing to worship the great-grandmother in her image of calf; once for not agreeing that there was only one manner of sexual congress; once for insulting what the grim ones said was an angel of their god come to the cities in search of even one righteous man.

And each time, in defiance of the laws, it was Banba who transported those who preferred challenging the unknown to staying in a familiar place and having the known visited upon them.

And where would she take them but to that place where the women who had survived the flood were living safe from the stern and cold ones, keeping themselves out of sight in the gentle valleys and hiding, not from fear but from prudence, in the hearts of the hills any time the outlanders came to explore or attempt to claim the soft green land.

The children of Dan, sometimes called the children of the goddess Danu, sometimes called the Danites, sometimes called the Danaanites, were welcomed by the women and their descendants, and in time they became as one people, often called the magic ones, the enchanted ones, the children of gods, or the Tuatha de Danaan.

And it was Banba who transported Fergus the Red to a new land. Fergus the Red was called so because of the colour of his hair, and he was a child in whom the urge to wander was strong. From the moment he could tuck his legs under him and stand upright on them, he explored, and when he was a young man, he informed the people he was not satisfied to stay where he had been born, but was moving on to a place he knew existed elsewhere, a place where he could rise in the morning and head off to see what he could see in a place he had not yet visited.

26

"Everything here," he said sadly, "I have visited two or even three times, and there is not one inch of this lovely place is not familiar to me."

Not a soul tried to discourage him for they wanted him to be happy, so why discourage him from travelling when it would only ensure his grief?

Scota, who had gone with Banba during her travels on the sea and who was the mother of Fergus, hugged him tightly and gave him food for his journey. "Do not forget us," she said, "and teach your children that we are all one people."

Fergus left with the most adventurous of the young people, and their adventures were many. The ship on which they travelled belonged to Banba, but Banba took her ship where Fergus asked, for it was his great adventure and not hers.

And when they arrived at the place Fergus known all along was there, he remembered how Scota had believed in his vision, and had given him comfort and food, and he named the place after her. He and his people headed off in one direction to fulfill their version of their destiny, and Banba set off in another direction to do what she had so enjoyed doing for so many years. At her side was a black bitch, the many many times great-granddaughter of that first loyal creature.

She visited the women of the North, with their thirteen massive pillars of stone. Thirteen menstrual cycles in a full year, and to not notice, not count, not honour these pillars meant instant death, for it signified an unbeliever without the ability to honour the creative life power. The northern women marked themselves with the sign of the crescent moon, tattooed on the brow above the nose, to tell all they honoured and served the Crone. They studied the known arts and sciences, and with each successful

completion of a course of study they had new designs
tattooed on their bodies. Those who were fully
qualified were covered with tattoos, the spiral of
eternity, the circle of life, the stylized representations
of the animals whose ways and wisdom they had
learned. And these tattooed women knew the secrets of
knots and ropes, the secret of the strangulation cords,
the secrets of using the human body as a weapon of
defence, and nobody who aspired to leadership in the
defence armies of the people could achieve their goal
without studying with these women. They could
change shape, could vanish from human sight, could
walk through walls and even stay alive while submerged in deep water.

Year after year, decade after decade, Banba travelled from the coasts to the mountains, along the rivers,
and through the valleys. She saw the great forests,
each tree so big it would take a dozen people with arms
outstretched to encircle it, and she saw the waters
teeming with fish, their bodies so closely packed a
person could walk across the stream on them, which
Banba and her dog often did. She met and had
conversations with all the magic people, she met and
had conversations with the goddesses, she discussed
things we could not begin to imagine, and things as
everyday as recipes and the best way to grow certain
crops. And she watched as the people who had gone
with Fergus moved out into their new land, marrying,
having children, living their lives and passing into the
arms of Ceridwen, the Crone, the collector, the
grandmother, the old hag, the one who gathers the
faithful to her. Ceridwen takes them where she can put
their poor dead bodies into her huge cauldron, then
make a soup, and the souls of the faithful are released
to rise with the steam, freed and healed, with neither
blemish nor fault. The soup is fed to the pack of black

bitches, the red-eyed black bitches who swarm at Ceridwen's feet and who race across the night skies doing her business, seeking the fallen faithful, sniffing out injustice, taking news of any evil done to women and children, then moving on Ceridwen's orders to avenge the harm done to the helpless or the vulnerable. The bones are lifted from the cauldron, rubbed dry, cleaned and polished, then given to Arianrhod, who uses them to enlarge the great loom on which she weaves the lives and destinies of mortals.

Banba learned to recognize the baying of the hounds of Ceridwen and to give them any message she had for the Crone, she learned to look to the Milky Way when addressing Arianrhod, she learned to dance the Maypole in honour of Creiddylad, she learned that when she looked to the sky and saw the rainbow she was seeing the cobweb robe of Kelle, which also shows in the night skies of winter and promises peace in paradise. She learned that it was the salmon, returning from uncharted seas to spawn in the rivers and streams, that first taught Boann the secrets of navigation, and that in the salmon is wisdom, and the power to see the future. She learned that Ceridwen, who is the great white sow, disguises herself often as the raven, in which guide she is the transformer, the one who brings or causes change. She learned that Ceridwen and the raven are protectors of bards, of poets, of musicians, and of seers, and that those who have studied certain skills and arts for half a long lifetime become not only raven but salmon.

Banba watched as the ones who had gone with Fergus began to identify themselves properly, began to realize that we all are equal in the tapestry of creation, with no thread more important than the other, and we are all knotted into our places equally. She watched as the ones who had brought with them seeds of madness

29

tried to subdue and control the earth's creatures. She watched as the one who would steal the power of the eagle was tricked and defeated by the magic of a sister, and she approved when the eagle accepted as cousins those who would honour that crest. She watched when the one who would have cut off the tail of the great red mare was stopped by magic and song, and she smiled when the horse, in honour and gratitude, accepted the friendship of humans and allowed them to claim her as cousin.

She watched it unfold, and saw every person claim a clan, until there were the people of the otter, the people of the bear, the people of the seal, the people of the wolf, the people of the hawk, the people of the wild boar, the people of even the small field mouse. And for each taking and naming there is a story, or even many stories, and if they are hidden, they are not forbidden, and can be found and reclaimed, can be again known and honoured. Banba herself was of the people of the horse, and of the people of the dog, she was of the people of the raven because of her knowledge of songs and stories, and, because of her long years of navigation, she was of the people of the salmon.

The four colours are red for the blood, white for the bone, yellow for the sun, and black for the night sky.

Banba laid stones in a circle, then laid other stones on top of those stones, then more stones and more until she had a conical hut made of stones and earth. Over this stone hut she piled more earth, and more earth, except for one place where she left a hole.

In this hut she built a fire. The smoke went up through the hole in the roof, the heat stayed in the stone walls, in the earth covering. Banba would go there and pray, would meditate and ponder, and would purify her body and her thoughts. The people watched, and learned, and soon they too built round sweat-houses of rock and earth, and with prayer and ritual they cleansed heart, soul, body, and mind.

$B$anba was visiting with the women of the North when the news came that ships had arrived and an army had invaded. Banba was no fool. She knew that any time there is an army on the loose, the best thing for ordinary people to do is assume a pacifism which is not passivity. And so she stayed out of the way of these legions.

For many years all she knew of them was that they seemed determined to cut down every tree in the land. The people tried to resist and were cut down, the people tried to fight and were slaughtered, and still the men came with the tools to destroy the forests and take the murdered trees back to their own country.

There were people in the land then who were dowsers, who knew the secrets of the earth, who could stand barefoot on the breast of the mother and determine what would best grow there, or whether it was land more suited to grazing or hunting than to crops. It was the dowsers who settled boundary disputes and found water, and it was the dowsers who walked the ley lines and knew their mysteries. The people believed the dowsers when they said that we are tied to the earth, connected to it as surely as is a tree, or the grass itself. With this knowledge, the people knew they had to defend the forests and keep the invaders from destroying the trees which were part of the earth herself.

And so the invaders moved against the dowsers. They gouged out their eyes so they could not see the beauty of the earth, they deafened their ears so they could not hear the song of creation, they slashed the tendons in their heels so they could not walk proud and strong upon the face of the earth, and then they cut out their tongues so they could not speak of what they knew; and when all that had been done, they took the children of the dowsers, slaughtered them, and hung their bleeding bodies around the shoulders and necks of their own parents.

Driven half mad by pain and more than mad by the anguish of knowing that their gift and treasure had caused the slaughter of their children, the dowsers were shoved and pushed along the ley lines they had once walked with such joy. Their agony was such that the earth herself roiled in protest and, to protect herself, withdrew from the crippled feet of the ones drenched in blood and shaking with pain. Our connection with the earth was severed, we began to lose the knowledge that we are part of, not apart from, all creation. And the great trees were cut and shipped off to be made into masts and decks for ships taking other legions to other lands to subjugate other people.

And Banba walked humbly among the people listening to their songs of sorrow. She grieved when the harpists were seized and their fingers smashed to stop the songs of protest, she wept when the fiddlers were taken and their elbows broken to silence the music that honoured Ceridwen, and she howled protest when the bards and poets were made mute that the stories of pride and tolerance be silenced. She watched as the people took the notes of the songs and hid them in the knots they twisted, in the patterns they wove and knit, and she prayed that one day the secrets would be uncovered, the knots and patterns would again become music.

Year after year horror and misery, and Banba kept herself out of it as much as she could. There were others who did as she did, and it does not matter whether they imitated her or she them, but some of the settled people, the Scaldie people, began to notice that the travelling Cairds managed never to be in one place long enough to be oppressed by the legions. If the legions marched to the north, the Cairds headed west; if the legions went west, the Cairds headed east or north. If Rome sent many groups out looking for the Cairds, they simply turned their herds of horses and cattle loose to forage for themselves on the moors, got into their small boats, and went visiting in Norway or Spain or Italy or wherever it was they could go and not encounter the mercenaries.

"Have you no pride?" some asked, "never to stand your ground and resist?"

"Pride," the Cairds laughed, "is cold comfort if you wind up buried in the ground, for there is no resisting the worms which will feast on your flesh."

"Only a coward," some said, "flees."

"Oh, fleas," the Cairds laughed, "great fleas have lesser fleas upon their backs to bite 'em, and lesser fleas have minor fleas and so on ad infinitum."

"And while you're being foolish and making jokes, the legions own your land!"

"Own? Own the land? And who can own a mountain and make the mountain believe in that ownership? Own? The land?" and the Cairds laughed happily.

Prasatagus was the consort of the queen of the Iceni people, the people of the horse, and to the legions this was interpreted as meaning he was king. Of course he was no such thing, only the one chosen to provide seed, but he too began to believe he was king, because the conqueror, Paulinus Suetonius, said so. Prasatagus made a pact with Paulinus Suetonius, to share with him the wealth

33

of the Iceni in return for protection from the legions.

The queen of the Iceni was a tall woman with strong legs from the years of riding horses, and strong arms from the years of practising with the weapons of defence. She had spent time with the northern women, and had even sent her youngest daughter to study with them. The queen had copper-coloured hair, and eyes that were sometimes blue, sometimes green, sometimes grey, changing as the sea itself changes, depending on her mood, depending on the weather, depending, even, on what colour clothes she wore. And she had a voice that was as harsh as the voice of a raven, as loud as the call of an angered sow, as rough as the bark on the trees the legions were cutting and hauling away, and Boadicea was not pleased with the bargain her consort had made. And so, after Prasatagus died, the queen of the Iceni went to Paulinus Suetonius under a banner of truce, to discuss with him the pact she had never made.

The legions did not honour the banner of truce. Instead, they took the queen and her two daughters captive. They took them to the top of a hill, where all the people could watch, and then tied the queen to a post and whipped her until the bones of her ribs showed through the great gashes in her skin, and she stood in a pool of her own blood. The legion stood ringed around the hill, and the people, on orders of their own bleeding queen, made no move to storm the hill, knowing that to defy her would mean their own deaths and the deaths of the queen and her daughters. So they were forced to watch and to mourn, singing their grief to give courage to their queen.

Then the legions staked out the two young girls and ravished them, repeatedly, man after man, ten after ten, hundred after hundred until the young princesses were incurably mad and more dead than alive.

Boadicea was forced to watch this, forced to hear this, forced to endure this, and her rage grew until her body glowed pink. When darkness fell she used her strong white teeth to gnaw through the lashings holding her to the splintered and blood-drenched post. She freed herself, throttled one of the guards, then used his knife to kill another guard. With a knife in each hand, she crept to where the legions were still raping her daughters, and with her heart breaking she threw the knives to stop the horror visited upon her children. Straight into each suffering heart a thrown knife, and their pain was finished, their horror over, their collection by Ceridwen assured.

The legions searched for Boadicea, but found no trace. She was gone as if she had never been in their hands.

And months later she reappeared, riding her wonderful horse Vindicator, her body scarred by the whip but as strong as ever it had been, and her voice made harsher than ever by the sobs grief had wrenched from her throat.

"I do not command you to fight," she told the people, "and it is for you to decide what you will do. But for myself, as a queen, as a woman, and as a mother, I will fight."

They rallied from every corner of the land. Not just the Iceni, not just the people of the horse, but the people of the dog, of the seal, of the otter, of the owl, of the hawk, of the wolf, of the bear, of the eagle, of even the small field mouse, and when they were ready, they attacked.

For the first time known in history, one entire legion was slaughtered and killed. Still the army of the people moved out, chasing the legions in front of them. They took back cities which had capitulated, and people who had co-operated with or aided the invaders were taken prisoner. Then, because it was a sin to spill the blood of a family member, they strangled them, leaving the blood unspilled but ensuring there would be no further betrayals. And the Cairds watched, and shook their heads, for they knew Rome would never allow such a thing to pass unavenged, or every conquered people would do the same and the might and power would be gone.

From every corner of the known world the legions were recalled and sent after the queen. Ship after ship, each of them unloading soldiers and mercenaries of every colour from every known land, all of them armed to the very teeth. And in one day of battle sixty thousand of the men, women, and children of the land were killed.

Suetonius claimed the queen herself had fallen and that her body had been hidden by the survivors to keep the legions from parading it as proof of their might. But Banba saw Boadicea arguing with her own people. Banba heard her say she would rather die in battle than flee, and she heard the people order their queen to mount Vindicator and ride away, and prepare for the day she would return and lead them again to victory. Banba watched as the queen struggled with her own will and then, as a true monarch should, allowed the wishes of her people to command her.

Paulinus Suetonius was in such a fury over the audacity of the Celtic people who had resisted, rebelled, and slaughtered his legion, that he went out into the land he called Gaul and laid waste to three quarters of it.

Every Celt who bore a scar was assumed to have received it in battle and was taken prisoner, then shipped in chains to Rome, to be tossed into the Coliseum to be a gladiator for the amusement of the crowds. Man or woman, young or old, each was handed a short sword and told to fight or die. And since it was unthinkable that sister should kill sister or brother kill brother or cousin kill cousin or anyone kill anyone with blood tie, they refused to fight against each other. Prisoners who did not know they were all children of the one great egg, those who did not know that the skin outside is no measure of difference, fought each other and died for no good reason at all.

And still Paulinus Suetonius was not content. He sent his madmen from one end of the country to the other and anything that was Celtic was taken. Infant children were stolen and given to Roman families to be taught Roman language, Roman customs, and Roman religion—to become, in short, Romans. Children too old to adapt fully to Roman ways were made slaves, taught to be stewards and servants, taught to administer for Rome but denied citizenship. The Celtic language was forbidden, Celtic religion was forbidden, Celtic music was forbidden, and the great stone carvings were smashed or taken on barges to the middle of the Channel and dumped into the sea. So much was destroyed that even the written language invented by Ogma, the Sun Faced One, the consort of the Mother, the father of Her children, was thought to be lost. It was not lost, however; it was given to the cranes and herons to protect and guard. Watch them as they fly, study the way their legs cross behind them, study the motion of their wings as they move against the line of the horizon, and you will see where the secrets of the sign language are hidden.

So violent and so bloody was the vengeance of Paulinus Suetonius that the Emperor could not tolerate the horror and had his Governor-General recalled.When the turmoil and lunacy had abated slightly, the Cairdic people were still travelling quietly from one end of the country to the other, training and trading horses, training and selling dogs, doing magic, playing music, juggling, and practising the healing arts.

"Bend as a willow," they advised, "or as the grass itself. Whoever tries to stand upright against a storm is apt to be broken."

The coming of the Roman legions and the destruction of the forests, the slaughter of the dowsers and the shattering of our connection to the earth, the violation of the waters and springs which were holy places, were accompanied by the arrival of the new religion. Thou Shalt Not Suffer A Witch To Live, they said, and if there was suffering, it was not they who did it but those they deemed to be witches.

Those with red hair were taken and torched, those with freckles were taken and burned, those who were different in any way, or who owned something another coveted, all were taken and burned. Women who owned their own property were accused and convicted. There was no rhyme or reason to it. Those who were guilty and those who were innocent, those who were thin and those who were fat, those who were and those who weren't were denounced, convicted, and set on fire.

Banba saw the beginning of it all and saved her skin by simply tucking her feet under her and slipping away on the boat she had disguised as fog.

She went to the Culdees and transported them to safety, she returned for the tattooed women and took them out of danger, and the brighter the witch-fires burned, the easier she could find her way back to take yet another load of those who would have become ash and carry them three months or more over the heaving sea.

Banba had learned from the Cairds and the Cairds

had learned from her that to the north and west lies freedom, and the grass grows everywhere.

It was a wonder that changed the course of history. It was progress and the proof of human intelligence, it has been honoured and continued; we know it as the Industrial Revolution.

Work once done at home by women became mechanized, huge machines were built and the people were sent to factories to work long hours for little pay. The machines gave and the machines demanded, and the cities were emptied of first the orphans, then the unwanted, then the children of the poor, and when there were no more orphans and the captains of industry needed a fresh supply, the people put their children to work before they were old enough to understand there was any other form of life.

But not the Cairds. They refused to allow their children into the factories, they refused to allow their children to be taken into the army or the navy, and if all else failed, they would slit the throats of their own children rather than have them slowly starved or mangled by machines.

They refused to pay taxes for, they said, we own nothing on which to pay any tax. They refused to join the army for, they said, generals are not part of our way of life. They refused to learn English or any language but their own, they refused to put their children in school to be educated in Scaldie ways or taught Scaldie manners. And so the Scaldies, for the good of the Cairds of course, gathered them up and transported them away from the land they had known since the days of Fergus, away from the paths they had trod all that time, to a land of which very little was known.

Banba went with the Cairds. She, who had travelled with St. Brendan the navigator, knew there was more to this new land than a few miles of farmland ruled by the authorities.

"No need to mourn," she encouraged them, "for we are the travelling people and in this new land we can travel our lifetimes and never see the same rock twice. If we start now and put one foot in front of the other for ten years we will not reach the other side!"

Live this way, do this, obey that, the Scaldie overseers said, and the Cairds agreed, nodded their heads, smiled, and at night they vanished.

Banba took her fog-mist boat and went back to see what she might see. Each time there were dispossessions she was there, a small white-haired woman, giving comfort, giving encouragement, whispering promises that were kept. And the Cairds who share a secret with the horses listened, the Cairds who can look at a dog and be its trusted friend looked at Banba and knew her as a woman of the people of the dog.

And still the displacements continued. The people were taken from their land and the land turned over for sheep, the people were marched at gunpoint by their own clan lords and put on ships to be taken across the sea to starve.

But there were those already in the new land who knew how to live there, and at night, while the guards and the authorities slept, others heard the beating of the drums and were gone before the sun showed her face again.

It might be they saw Boadicea on Vindicator, calling to them with her harsh raven's-caw voice, or it might be that a small-bodied woman with white hair came to them and whispered a promise they knew she would keep. They moved ahead of authority, away from authority, in spite of authority, and at times into authority, and they took their songs, their laughter, their wit, their irreverence, their ever-evolving tales and stories.

And you must beware. They move among us and sing of subversion, they move among us looking like us and telling tales of disrespect. They joke about things decent people consider serious, they have no respect for what proper people consider important, and they are the people about whom you have been warned.

They move among you and tell you to honour the earth, they move among you and tell you to respect the forests, they move among you and speak of clean rivers and streams, they move among you and remind you of how it once was and can be again. They tell enormous tales of shape-shifters and form-changers, they sing songs that mock the laws of the land, they are in your churches and in your schools and they are the people about whom you have been warned.

Their men are dangerous and not to be trusted. They respect their wives and daughters, their mothers and sisters. They think fighting is foolish and armies insane. They will do no work that damages or injures the fullness of creation, and they have been known to openly express their feelings. Their women are abominations who think for themselves, who earn their own money and claim their own children, who refuse to be docile and who dress as they please and they are the people about whom you have been warned.

And, of course, none of this is true. There are few references in any respectable scholarly work of a people known as the Cairds. There is no dictionary in any recognized institution in which their language is laid out for anyone to study and understand. They never moved as they wished across the face of the land, they never told their stories only to those who understood Gaelic, they never resisted oppression by laughing and moving on, and that is why even today there are laws in Britain which restrict the right of the travelling people to park more than one caravan on any piece of land at one time.

None of it is true. You cannot stand on your front porch at night and stare up at the moon and see Banba's white hair wisping cloud-like across the dark sky. You will never see a woman with white hair who catches your eye and commands you with her gaze, then smiles as if you, like the horses, share a secret with her. You will never see a woman with white hair accompanied by a strong black bitch and you will never look at clean pure water and know in your heart why it is precious.

None of it is true. There are no people about whom you have been warned, and if there were, they would not be the Cairds. They have all died off and anyway they never existed. It is nothing but stories, and stories are lies, as are songs, and poems, and promises of truth.

# THE SACRED POOL

There was once a widow with three sons and a daughter. The sons learned the sciences of war, the daughter studied the arts of harp-playing and the telling of stories.

One day the daughter found a bear lying in a thicket, its face terribly swollen and infected. An arrowhead was lodged in its face, the tip stuck in the jawbone, and the poor beast could not open her mouth to eat or drink. Though the bear was close to death and could not open her mouth to bite, she still had long sharp claws and was capable of using them. Every time the young woman moved, the bear growled a warning and lifted her paws.

The girl unslung her harp, sat near the thicket, and began to play a gentle song. Within minutes, the poor sick bear was fast asleep, lulled by the music. The young woman took her small sharp silver knife, cut open the infected jaw, and cleaned the wound, but the arrowhead was too firmly lodged for her to pull it out with her fingers.

She loosened a silver string from her harp, slipped it

around the arrowhead, tightened the string, braced herself, and pulled as hard as she could. The sleeping bear groaned, the young woman pulled hard a second time, and the arrowhead popped out. Cleansing blood began to flow and the great bear lurched to her full height, towering above the terrified young woman.

"Hush, hush," the girl managed, "hush and I'll tell you a story."

The bear hesitated, then sat back down on the soft mossy earth and the young woman told the bear a story:

> Two sisters went to gather fruit, but as fast as Moorachug picked, that fast did Meenachug eat, and finally Moorachug became angry and went to a tree to cut a good stick.
>
> "What do you want?" asked the tree.
>
> "A good strong stick to beat my sister who eats all the fruit as fast as I pick it."
>
> "You will never cut that stick," said the tree, "until you find an axe made of silver to harvest that branch." Moorachug reached for an axe made of silver, but the axe pulled away from her hand.
>
> "You cannot use me until you find a stone to sharpen my blade," said the axe. So she went to where she knew there were sharpening stones, and reached to get one to sharpen the axe to cut the branch to beat her sister who ate all the fruit.
>
> "You cannot use me," the sharpening stone said, "until you find water to wet me." So she went to the stream to get water to wet the stone to sharpen the axe to cut the branch to beat her sister who ate all the fruit.
>
> "You cannot use me," said the water, "until you find a fine white doe to swim across me." So Moorachug went looking for a fine white doe to

swim the water to wet the stone to sharpen the axe to cut the branch to beat her sister who ate all the fruit.

"You cannot catch me," the fine white doe said, "until you get a dog to run me down." And Moorachug went looking for a good strong dog to chase the fine white doe to swim the water to wet the stone to sharpen the axe to cut the branch to beat her sister who ate all the fruit.

"I will not do it," said the dog, "until you get butter to rub on my feet." And she went looking for butter to rub on the feet of the good strong dog to chase the fine white doe to swim the water to wet the stone to sharpen the axe to cut the branch to beat on her sister who ate all the fruit.

"You will not have me," said the butter, "until you find a little grey mouse to lick the plate clean." She went in search of a little grey mouse to lick clean the butter to rub on the feet of the good strong dog to chase the fine white doe to swim the water to wet the stone to sharpen the axe to cut the branch to beat her sister who ate all the fruit.

"You cannot catch me," said the mouse, "without a cat with long whiskers and tail." Moorachug went in search of a cat with long whiskers and tail to catch the grey mouse to lick clean the butter to rub on the feet of the good strong dog to chase the fine white doe to swim the water to wet the stone to sharpen the axe to cut the branch to beat her sister who ate all the fruit.

"I will not go," said the cat, "until you give me a bowl of rich cream." She went in search of good rich cream to give to the cat with long whiskers and tail to catch the grey mouse to lick clean the butter to rub on the feet of the good strong dog to chase the fine white doe to swim the water to wet the stone to sharpen the axe to cut the branch to beat her sister who ate all the fruit.

"No milk or cream for you," said the cow, "until you get me some hay from the stable boy." And Moorachug went in search of the stable boy to get the hay to feed the cow to get the cream to give to the cat with the long whiskers and tail to catch the grey mouse to lick clean the butter to rub on the feet of the good strong dog to chase the fine white doe to swim the water to wet the stone to sharpen the axe to cut the branch to beat her sister who ate all the fruit.

"No hay for you," said the stable boy, "until you get me some bannock from the kitchen cook." She went in search of the kitchen cook to get the bannock to give to the stable boy to get the hay to feed the cow to get the cream to give to the cat with the long whiskers and tail to catch the grey mouse to lick clean the butter to rub on the feet of the good strong dog to chase the fine white doe to swim the water to wet the stone to sharpen the axe to cut the branch to beat on her sister who ate all the fruit.

"No bannock for you," said the kitchen cook, "until you bring in some water to knead the bannock." So Moorachug went in search of water to give to the kitchen cook to get the bannock to give to the stable boy to get the hay to feed the cow to get the cream to give to the cat with the long whiskers and tail to catch the grey mouse to lick clean the butter to rub on the feet of the good strong dog to chase the fine white doe to swim the water to wet the stone to sharpen the axe to cut the branch to beat on her sister who ate all the fruit.

"Take the bucket, you silly girl." So she took the bucket to get the water to give to the kitchen cook to get the bannock to give to the stable boy to get the hay to feed the cow to get the cream to give to the cat with the long whiskers and tail to catch the grey mouse to lick clean the butter to rub on the feet of the good strong dog to chase the fine white doe to swim the water to wet the stone to sharpen the axe to cut the branch to beat her sister who ate all the fruit.

Moorachug dipped the bucket and got the water, but the bucket leaked and the water drained out. "What will I do?" she wailed. "I need the water to give to the cook to get the bannock to give to the stable boy to get the hay to feed the cow to get the cream to give to the cat with the long whiskers and tail to catch the grey mouse to lick clean the butter to rub on the feet of the good strong dog to chase the fine white doe to swim the water to wet the stone to sharpen the axe to cut the branch to beat my sister who ate all the fruit."

"Fool, fool, fool," called a raven. "In the time you have wasted in this round-about search you could have picked all the fruit from all the trees and all the berries from all the bushes and nobody could possibly have eaten all of that! Mix moss and mud and fix the hole!"

So she picked moss and mud and mixed the two, then plugged the hole. She took the water to the kitchen cook who made some bannock for the stable boy who ate the bannock and gave the hay and the cow ate the hay and gave some cream and the cat with the long tail and whiskers drank the cream and caught the grey mouse to lick clean the butter to rub on the feet of the good strong dog to chase the fine white doe to swim the water to wet the stone to sharpen the axe and she finally cut the branch to beat her sister who ate all the fruit.

She returned to the orchard with the fine strong stick and found that her sister had BURST.

The bear shook her head at the folly of humankind, then yawned, lay down her poor damaged head, and fell asleep. Every day the young woman visited the bear, brought her food, cleaned the wound, and sang songs to bring rest and sleep to the tortured animal.

She arrived one morning to find that the bear had given birth to three cubs: a black one, a red fox-coloured one, and a white one. The girl cuddled the babies and stroked them, rocked them and fussed over them, telling the mother bear how beautiful they were. She even brought milk from her own herd of goats to help feed the hungry little things.

When the cubs were older and hungry all the time, the girl took them scraps from the kitchen because the mother bear was still not strong enough to travel through the forest and hunt for their food.

Finally the time came when the huge brown bear with the great ugly scar along her jaw was healed and ready to leave.

"It was a young man with a bow and arrow who nearly killed me and my three unborn cubs," said the brown bear, "and as I lay dying I hated all people. But then you came, and here we are, all four of us alive and healthy."

"I'm afraid it was my brother, practising the sciences of war," the young woman admitted.

"You are not responsible for what he does," the bear said, "and if you or any of yours need any help from me or any of mine, you have only to call and we will come."

The girl kissed the bear, then she taught the cubs a little dance and gave it to them as a farewell gift, and they parted to go their separate ways.

Some time later, bringing her herd of goats back

after a day of strolling along the banks of the stream, she came across her second brother setting nets between the trees.

"Why?" she asked, greatly puzzled.

"I am going to catch an eagle," her brother said, "and when it is caught, I will kill it and stuff it and set it on a pole as a sign to all that I am not as others. I will get the far-seeing eyes of an eagle and soar above all other men as the eagle soars above the earth, and when they see my standard they will be afraid and my army will win all the battles."

"What a cruel and stupid thing," she said, but he laughed at her and told her to go away because she understood nothing of the science of war and was only good for the arts of playing the harp and telling daft tales.

She was up before the others the next day. As usual she milked her goats, put the milk in the kitchen, then took her animals out to browse on the tender shoots along the riverbank. In the net her brother had strung was a dead eagle and near it, a second eagle, wings flapping, feet caught in the webbing of the cruel trap. Mourning for the dead bird, the girl took her little silver knife and cut free the second one.

"I'm sorry," she said, "it was my brother set the net."

"Curse him and his kind," the eagle said. "He has left me a widow and my children will starve, for it takes us both, hunting full time, to get enough mice, rats, and fish to feed them."

That night the young woman set out milk and cheese. The rats and mice all came to feast, but the milk and cheese were set out in traps and the next day the young woman took a basket of rodents to the grieving eagle. The young ones were so hungry they tumbled each over the other in their eagerness to get the food, and the young woman laughed. The eagle was amazed at the sound, and while the young eagles feasted, the young woman taught the mother eagle how to laugh.

Every night she set out traps, and every day she took mice and rats to feed the young. When they were grown and ready to fly, the mother eagle said to the girl, "If ever you or any of yours have need of me or any of mine, you have but to call and we will be there, from now until the very last day of time."

The girl never told her brother she had freed an eagle, and kept the secret in her heart.

The third brother gathered all his men and sent them out to build a great fence from one end of the forest to the other, and when the fence was built, he set the forest afire. All the animals ran from the fire, only to come up against the great stone fence. They ran along the fence looking for a way out, and found at the end of it a huge field with a fence all around and an enormous gate standing open to let them run inside. The animals ran away from the fire, through the great gate, and into the field, and the brother and his men swung shut the great gate, trapping the animals.

"The world will see," the brother boasted, "that I am the greatest hunter of all. I will wear the horns of the stag and my banner will be the cut-off tail of the great red mare."

The girl took up her harp and played a song for rain, which fell at her request and quenched the terrible fire. Then she played a song for sleep. Her brother and all his men fell to the grass and closed their eyes. Then she tried to cut the lashings holding the gate shut, but her little silver knife was no match for the hinges.

"Bear, oh bear," she cried, and the great brown bear with the wicked scar along her jaw was there in a flash with her three variously coloured cubs. Wham bam slam smash and the gate was down.

"Eagle, oh eagle," the girl cried, and the eagle was

there to lead the animals away from the charred forest and trampled field, lead them to a place where they could live free and safe.

As the great red mare moved through the opening where the gate had been, she stopped and nudged the girl with her huge head. "They would have cut off my tail to be a banner," she said, "and used my hide to cover their shields. If you ever have need of me or any of mine, you have but to ask and we will reply."

The great stag and his doe stopped, too, and nodded their heads in greeting. "They would have taken my antlers and worn them on their helmets. If you ever have need of me or any of mine, you have but to let us know and we will be there."

The wolf and otter stopped and said the same thing, and then it was the turn of the great black bitch of the night. She was swollen with puppies and still panting from the terrible chase, but she sniffed at the girl's hand and licked her fingers in greeting. "I would have been dead and my unborn young, too," she said, "but you have saved us. I never thought people would do any of us wild ones a good turn and I am glad you have proved me wrong. I and mine will be at your side any time we are needed, from now until the last day of time."

When all the animals were gone and safe, even the slow-moving mole, even the snake which crawls, the young woman went home, leaving that brother and his men sleeping, their weapons rusting in the rain.

The rain stopped and the sun shone, but many animals and birds had died in the fire, and a pestilence grew because of it. The uncles of the young woman died, and her mother lay ill and dying. The herb woman said that only clean water could save her life, and that water must come from the place where all the water in the world bubbles up from a blessed spring.

51

"Well," said the brothers, "we are the ones who will get it for her. We know the sciences of war, and if anyone should interfere with us, we will chop off his head!" They called together their armies and headed off, stopping at the bewitched meadow to try to waken the third brother. He and his men lay in the grass, breathing slowly and regularly, as healthy as ever they had been. But nothing anyone said or did could waken them, so they were left there with their weapons ruined, gone rusty, dull, and useless.

Days passed, then weeks, and the mother was neither sicker than she had been nor cured of the disease, but there was no sign of either of the sons.

The daughter fretted. She cared for her flocks and herds, she sat up at night with her sick mother, and she worried.

"Oh girl who is almost a woman," cried the raven, "will you sit forever waiting for someone else to do what only you can do?"

"I have never been farther away from home than a morning's gentle stroll," the girl protested. "I know nothing of the world beyond!"

"You will never be any younger than you are now," the raven mocked.

"But I know nothing!"

"You won't learn any younger!" the raven repeated.

The daughter sat under a hawthorn tree and thought deeply about all that had happened, and knew if anyone was to find and return with the magic water of life from the end of the world, it would have to be she herself. She packed a few necessaries, slung her harp over her shoulder, kissed her ailing mother goodbye, and set off in search of that which might save the life of the person most dear to her in all the world.

The very first large city she reached was the place she found her two brothers. They had gone only as far

as the first plentiful supply of intoxicating liquors, and
there they stopped with their men, all of them drinking,
gambling, brawling, and being as foolish as anyone
ever was.

"I thought you were on a quest!" she scolded.

"Tuck your feet under you, little sister," they answered bitterly, "or you will be very sorry!"

"Your mother lies ill and you amuse yourselves?"

"If you don't shove off, we'll amuse ourselves by
lifting your head from your shoulders!"

She shook her head, sucked her teeth, and walked
away from them, leaving them to their tankards of ale
and their gambling.

She walked through meadows and through fields, she
walked past thickets and past streams until, at night-
fall, she came to an enormous forest of brooding trees,
their roots deep in the soil, their branches reaching for
the sky, their trunks so big around that thirteen women
joining hands could not have encircled the smallest
one.

She was about to settle herself for sleep when, with a
great crashing and smashing, an enormous black bear
approached, and in its mouth was a small stone bowl,
and in the bowl a gleaming coal. Quicker than she
thought she could, the girl was out of her blanket and
clambering up the closest tree, her harp safe with her.

The bear sat on the girl's blanket, put the stone bowl
on the ground, and stared up into the tree.

"Come down," she said.

"No," the girl replied.

"Come down," the bear repeated, "or I'll go up after
you."

"Better that," the girl replied, "than that I volunteer to
climb down into your great mouth full of sharp white
teeth!"

"I don't intend to eat you," the bear answered. "I need

your help." And the bear stood and bowed clumsily. "Oh little dance teacher." The bear moved awkwardly in the steps the girl had taught the tiny cubs.

"Why, it's you!" the girl exclaimed, coming down the tree. She embraced the bear happily, although it was so big her arms could only close around its head.

"I have this piece of fire in this bowl," the bear mourned, "but I have no hands, only paws, and I cannot make a proper fire."

Quicker than it takes to tell, the girl gathered twigs, leaves, and sticks, then dumped the glowing coal into the pile. Just that easily, they had a warm, cheery fire.

"You could drag such material to the mouth of your den," the girl instructed, "and lay the coal in some dry moss. Then all you have to do is keep dry wood on hand, keep the fire going all the time, and you will have it when you need it."

"Like the story you told my mother," the black bear laughed. "Cause and effect, cause and effect, for every cause at least one effect, for every effect at least one cause."

The bear decided that now that there was a fire, they needed something to cook. Off she went, returning shortly with a fine young stag. "Do you know how to cook?" she asked hopefully. "When I was small you would bring us scraps, and I learned to love the taste of cooked meat. But I myself am ignorant of the art."

"See," the girl demonstrated, "close enough to the fire to cook, not so close as to burn, and turn it often so it bastes in its own juice."

When the meat was cooked, they sat together eating until both of them were stuffed, and only the bones remained.

"Sleep," the great black bear said. "Sleep between my paws. I will keep you warm all night." The young woman lay down between the huge front paws of the

54

great black bear, and they slept warm together, like two sisters sharing the same comfortable bed. In the morning they buried the bones in a pit the black bear dug, and no sooner had the pit been filled in and covered than four young stags sprang from it and raced away free, into the forest.

"Climb on my back," the bear offered, "and hang on!" The girl climbed on, gripping with legs, hands, and at times even her teeth, and the bear took off through the forest, across the meadow, and over the stream.

As night began to fall, they came to a large plain castle built of rock and earth. "Go inside," the bear said, "and when the greogagh who lives in the house asks who you are and why you dare disturb her, tell her that it is the black bear who sent you."

She kissed the black bear goodbye, walked up boldly, and knocked on the door.

"And who are you?" asked the greogagh.

"I am she who asks for shelter," replied the girl.

"Why ask here?" the swarthy forest-dweller asked suspiciously. "You are of the race who chases me and my children, who cut the trees and put metal where a poor little greogagh child might step on it and be seriously burned. We have told you and told you that the mess you leave scattered everywhere is poison to us, we have told you even one small nail can burn us so badly we are crippled for life, and yet every day the discarded metal tools and artifacts are left where we cannot avoid them, and every day we are forced to move farther away from the places where we have always lived."

"Oh, greogagh, what can I say?" the girl answered. "I myself try not to leave a mess behind, but it is true there are others who seem not to care."

"And why would you think I would be inclined to help you?"

"The great black bear of the forest told me to come to this house and ask for shelter," the girl answered.

The greogagh opened the door and stepped aside to allow the girl to enter. The rock and earth had no windows, only openings and holes to let in fresh air and light. The greogagh has no knowledge of fire, so there was none, and the castle was cold and damp. The greogagh is not bothered by cold or damp, for she has a fine brown pelt on her body, and long brown hair falling from her round head, down her back and over her shoulders.

"If it is the great black bear sent you," the greogagh said quietly, "then you are welcome."

The meal the young woman shared with the greogagh was nothing at all like the one she had shared with the bear. There was neither meat nor fish nor anything cooked, only seeds and berries, grains and greens. "If you grind the grain," the girl said, "you can make flour, and with flour you can make bread."

"Ah," the greogagh smiled, her large round brown eyes crinkling at the corners, "but you need fire, and an oven."

"We could use stones," the young woman offered, "and build a small hearth."

"Yes," the greogagh agreed, "and then the smoke would rise to the sky and show those who chase us where we live. They will trap us in metal traps, even kill us."

"Then," the young woman decided, "once I have found that for which I search, and my mother is well, and I am home again, know that there will be no metal left scattered around to harm you, nobody will chase you, and any time you come to visit us, we will give you bread. And cheese," she promised, "and milk and sweet cakes."

"When you are home again," the greogagh vowed, "I

will come to visit. And if I like the taste of what you can provide, I will stay a while and work in your gardens." She smiled and nodded her head happily. "Any garden tended by a greogagh gives more than twice the usual harvest."

The young woman unslung her silver harp, making sure that no part of it touched the greogagh, and then she played and sang to repay the kindness shown her. The greogagh listened, enthralled, making happy soft sounds deep in her throat. When the young woman put aside the harp and took off her silver knife, the greogagh pulled out the straw-filled pallet, and they slept together like sisters, warm under a thick blanket of moss and straw.

In the morning it was the great fox-red bear who was waiting to transport the young woman over hill and dale, over stream and creek, and as night began to fall, they camped by the banks of a river. The young woman and the fox-red bear caught fish, grilled them on sticks over the fire the girl had made, and had their fill of silver-sided salmon. They dug a pit for the heads, tails, fins, and bones, and filled it up again. As had happened with the bones of the stag, four times the number of fish they had eaten streamed from the hole and splashed back into the water.

Then, from that same water, another creature emerged. The great fox-red bear retreated, growling warning deep in her throat. The ech-ushkya looked at the young woman and saw she was not afraid; the young woman looked at the ech-ushkya and saw a water horse, a handsome grey and silver creature with blue-glinting eyes.

"And would you like a ride?" the ech-ushkya asked.

"No," said the girl. "You want me to believe you are a kelpie, but the kelpie always wears a magic bridle. And if a person climbs upon a kelpie and the kelpie goes back into the water, a person can dismount and swim back to shore. But ech-ushkya wears no bridle, and, once on, a person cannot dismount, so is taken into the water, drowned, and then eaten."

"Oh," laughed the water horse, "do I look like an animal who would do a thing like that to a young woman like yourself? Here, you have but to stroke my forehead and you will know that I am no threat to you." The animal pushed its head forward, but before it could touch the girl, a young black bitch leapt from the thicket and closed her sharp white teeth on the ech-ushkya's nose. The creature gave a screech of surprise and pain, turned itself back to water, and drained into the stream again with a sucking, slithering noise.

"Never let the ech-ushkya touch you," the young black bitch warned. "And if it tries, grab its nose and pinch. It cannot stand to be grasped in any way, and as soon as something closes around it, be it the nose, the leg, or the ears, it turns into water and is gone."

"You will be safe with the black dog," the fox-red bear said, "and in the morning you will have help." And the shy bear headed for the forest, stopping only briefly to do a few steps of the little dance the girl had taught her as a small cub.

The young woman slept wrapped in her cloak with the black dog pressed against her back, keeping watch and guarding her the whole night.

In the morning it was the white bear waiting for her. "Climb on my back," the bear invited.

"Thank you," the girl answered, and climbed on the back of the great white bear, clinging to its fur with hands and even teeth.

"Hang on tight," the bear warned, "for today we must climb." And climb they did, up the slopes of the mountains, up past the place where the trees grow, up even past the place where the grass, the heather, and the small flowers grow, up until there was only snow and ice, and more snow and ice.

Then they were at the place where all the water of the earth is born. There was a deep oval cleft in the rocks, and from it a crystal clear spring bubbled strongly, tinged with the blue of the sky, foaming with the speed of its own surging.

The bear knelt and the girl dismounted, but before she could fill even one bladderskin with the water, a pack of black dogs sprang from the earth and surrounded the holy spring, their bright red eyes blazing, their sharp white fangs gleaming.

"Well, then," said the girl, "kill me if you must, but I will die rather than run from you."

The furious dogs just stood their ground, glaring. The young woman unslung her harp and played every song she knew, but the dogs ignored the music and stood ready to defend the spring. The animals she had helped came to assist her, and each of them spoke of her courage and kindness. Still the black dogs would not move.

"Well, if I must die, I must die," she said sadly. She moved toward the spring and the dogs snarled. "Only death will keep me from collecting these three bladderskins of water," she told them, "for it is my mother needs it to save her life."

"And how will clean, pure water save her life?" asked the head dog.

The girl confessed the family shame. "The water in our land was poisoned after my brother committed an evil act. Because of what he did, the water became foul, and my mother lies in that no-place place between life and death. The herb woman says only clean, pure water will save her life, and I will do whatever I must do to save the life of my mother."

"A brave and noble thing," the head dog said. The wild red glare faded from his eyes, his lips came down to cover his fangs, his snarl vanished, and he looked like any dog in the world, except that when he moved, his toe-claws did not click on the rocks.

The young woman filled her three bladderskins with water from the sacred pool where all the water of earth springs from the ground. Then she thanked the dogs for allowing her passage, and thanked all of the animals who had pleaded on her behalf. She climbed on the back of the white bear, the waterskins dangling from her shoulders, her hands, fingers, and even her teeth gripping tightly, and they sped back down from the cold mountain peak.

Down they went past the ice and snow to the place where the heather and the small flowers bloom, down past where the grass grows, down into the trees, down, down to the valley and the river that flows there, fed from the blessed spring.

They stopped for the night and the young woman started a fire and cooked fish they caught in the river. When they had eaten, they again buried what they could not use, and again a torrent of silvery-sided fish sprang from the burial pit and leapt into the water.

As the fish splashed into the water, the earth opened and a great cave was revealed. Without hesitation, the young woman went into the cave. Strange and wonderful icicles of stone and crystal hung from the ceiling and sprang from the floor, and the light from the cooking fire was reflected a million times. On a stone table, the young woman found a bottle of wine and a glass. She filled the glass with wine and offered it to the white bear, then to the black dog, who still accompanied her, and then to the eagle. When it was time to refill the glass, the girl found that the bottle remained full.

"Take it," said the bear, "for if it was not intended for you, it would empty itself."

The young woman took the bottle of wine and moved deeper into the cave, to a second room in which stood another table, this one of wood. On it was a long loaf of fine crusty white bread. The young woman cut a slice for the bear, a slice for the dog, a slice for the eagle, and a slice for herself, but though they ate the bread, the loaf remained whole.

"Take it," said the eagle. "If it was not intended for you, it would turn to crumbs."

In a third room the young woman found another table, this one made of silver, and on it lay a great round of cheese. She cut cheese for the bear, for the dog, for the eagle, and for herself, and though they ate generous helpings of the cheese, it remained a full round, as if not a crumb of it had been taken.

"Take it," said the dog. "If it was not intended for you, it would disappear."

In a fourth room she found a woman lying asleep, and when she went to waken her, the animals told her to leave the woman undisturbed. "She will waken when it is time and she is needed," they told her.

"But if the wine, the bread, and the cheese belong to her, what will she have when she wakens?" the girl demanded.

The animals just looked at her. The dog asked, "Is it any of your concern? Who is she to you? Why would you care?"

The young woman went back to the table of silver and replaced the cheese. "I cannot take this," she said, "for if the beautiful woman wakens, she will need food."

No sooner had she replaced the cheese than two rounds of cheese stood in its place. The second round said, "I will stay here," while the first one said, "I will go with you." The young woman gladly took the offer of the cheese, but moved back to the second table, the one made of wood. On it she put the loaf of bread. "I cannot take the bread," she said, "for if the beautiful woman wakens, she will be hungry." Immediately the bread became two loaves, and the second loaf said, "I will stay," while the first loaf said, "I will go with you."

Back toward the entrance they went, and at the first table, the one made of stone, the young woman replaced the bottle of wine.

"And if she wakens, she will be thirsty," she said. "It would be theft and cruelty to deny her the wine which is hers by right." And then there were two bottles on the table, the second one saying, "I will stay," the first one saying, "I will go with you."

They left the cave and spent the night beside the warm fire. In the morning they saved some coals for the next night, put out the fire and buried the embers and ashes, then set off, the girl riding on the back of the eagle.

They were flying over rich farmland when the eagle first noticed a long line of people winding their way toward a castle set atop a small knoll. The eagle circled the small knoll, studying the throng of heavily bur-dened people. The cavalcade went in through the front gate leading cows, sheep, goats, horses, and pigs, carry-ing chickens, ducks, pigeons, even geese, dragging wagons loaded with oats and wheat, barley and flax. But when they came from the back gate, their hands were empty and their pockets turned inside out.

The eagle landed on the grass and the young woman dismounted.

"What is that place?" she asked one of the unhappy people.

"It is the castle of the giant one-eyed fomor," the villager replied. "He forces us to give our crops and livestock to him. If we refuse, he comes from his castle and lays waste to the land, uprooting trees, trampling houses, ruining our fields, and talking all that we own anyway. Better to give him what he wants and live in poverty and peace, than deny him and live in poverty and grief."

The young woman went into the castle as brave and bold as if it were her very own home, and she marched up to the giant one-eyed fomor.

"You!" she shouted up at him. "Why do you treat these people so badly?"

"Badly?" the one-eyed fomor replied. "I stay in my castle, I do not trample their fields or smash their houses, I do not uproot their orchards or break the bridges and fences; how badly are they treated?"

"You take everything they can grow," she answered, "leaving them little for themselves."

"Then they can grow or raise more!" the fomor bellowed. "Not a one of them is as hungry as I am! There is never enough food for me, and every year they bring me less."

"They bring less because they have less, you great idiot," the young woman shouted. "If you kill and eat all the mares, who will mother the next year's foals? If you kill and eat the cows, from where will you get calves? If the hens have been eaten, who will lay the eggs or hatch the chicks? Here!" She tossed the one-eyed giant the loaf of bread. "Try to eat that, you ever-hungry maw!"

The fomor began to eat the loaf, but however much he ate, still the loaf remained whole.

"See how much of this you can devour," called the girl, tossing him the round of cheese. Again the Fomor gobbled hungrily, and again the cheese was not diminished.

"Take this," she said, passing him the bottle of wine.

The giant drank the wine, smacked his lips, and ate more of the bread and cheese.

"If you promise to leave these poor people alone," the young woman said, "I will give you the loaf, the cheese, and the wine. You will always have enough food and drink, you will never again be hungry. And," she said cannily, "perhaps if you offer to lend your great strength whenever there is a big job to be done—a dam to build or a boulder to be taken from a field—then perhaps these people will from time to time bring you a young ram to roast."

"I could just keep them," the one-eyed fomor laughed, "and send you on your way with a bruise where I slapped your ear."

"You could try," she agreed, "but if you do, the loaf will become crumbs, the cheese will become rind, and the wine will turn to vinegar."

"One ram from time to time is not very much," the fomor grumbled, "and a person could get tired of only bread and cheese."

"Two minutes ago you complained of hunger; now you are not happy with good plain food. Look at you! Sitting on a great throne of gold, up to your knees in diamonds, rubies, emeralds, and pearls, with silver and gold coins heaped in the corners, while these poor people have no treasure of any kind, only the fruit of their toil and the sweat of their brow. Why not offer to buy their surplus?"

"Buy their surplus?" the giant gaped in wonder.

"Buy their surplus," she said firmly. "Then they would be able to go to the city and buy more of what they need. And you would have food without having to terrorize your neighbours."

When the young woman again flew off on the wings of the eagle, she had her silver knife, her silver harp, and the three bottles of pure water from the source of all the water in the world, but the loaf, the cheese, and the wine stayed with the fomor.

When they reached the very room where her brothers had last been seen drinking and gambling, the young woman kissed her friends goodbye, promised them a place at her hearth whenever they wished to visit, and went into the city to find her brothers. And find them she did. The days of song and laughter were finished for the brothers; they had lost their youth, their money, and their health, and the only way they had of getting food was to beg for it on the streets.

The young woman was sorely tempted to leave them there, but she knew her poor mother would never rest, wondering about the two errant sons. So she took pity on them, using her own money to buy them food and drink and a hot bath and new clothes. When they were clean, warm, and fed, she told them she was going back home with the water their mother needed. Since she could so obviously look after them better than they could look after themselves, the brothers decided to accompany her.

But when they were almost home, the two brothers conspired to steal the jugs of water and claim they had found it themselves. They hit their sister on the head with rocks and sticks until she was unconscious and threw her in the ditch. Then the two villains took the three bladderskins of water and hurried on to their mother's house, where they claimed to have found the holy spring.

Meanwhile the girl lay in the ditch, rain falling on her face, her body growing colder and colder. She tried to rise, but couldn't. She tried to crawl from the ditch, but her body refused to obey her. She knew then that she was very close to death.

"Oh mother," she prayed, "I know that everyone dies sooner or later, but I grieve that I will never get to see you healthy again, and that I will not be able to kiss you one last time. But if the water cures you of your illness, then even this death in a ditch is worth it."

Suddenly she felt warm, as if the sun were aimed at her, and a voice whispered in her ear.

"Where is the wine? Where is the bread? Where is the cheese?"

"I gave it to the one-eyed fomor," the girl answered, "so he would stop his oppression of the people."

Then she felt a soft hand under her poor broken head, and the pain vanished. Her eyes could see, strength returned to her body, and she could sit up again, warmth revitalizing her.

"Oh," she gasped. 'Oh, it's you, who were asleep in the cave!"

The magic woman smiled, kissed the girl on the cheek, and helped her from the bitterly cold water of the ditch.

"What do you remember most about the cave?" she asked.

"The great crystals hanging from the ceiling and growing up from the floor," the girl answered.

"Come with me," the magic woman said, "and we will see what we will see."

The girl and the magic woman started along the road. Suddenly the girl's filthy wet clothes were gone. She wore, instead, soft leather pants, a soft white shirt, and a beautiful green woven vest decorated with embroidered spirals and designs. Most magical of all, from a silver chain around her neck hung a great glittering crystal which caught the light of the sun and broke it into every colour ever seen.

The magic woman snapped her fingers and two horses appeared, one white and one red. The magical woman swung onto the back of the white one, the girl climbed on the back of the great red mare, and they rode forward, accompanied by a pack of silent black dogs.

At the home of the young woman's mother, the brothers were trying to open the bladderskins to prove they had found the holy water. But no matter how hard they pulled, the stoppers would not come out, and no blade in the house could slit open the skins.

Suddenly the room was full of red-eyed silent black dogs, swarming and pushing, knocking the bladderskins from the hands of the villains, standing between them and that which they would have stolen. The brothers backed into a corner and stood trembling, exposed as cowards to all eyes. Two figures moved toward the bed where the mother lay ill. The magic woman nodded, and one of the dogs brought a bladderskin to the hands of the one who had made the journey and found the holy spring. The young woman easily pulled the stopper from the bladderskin and gave her mother pure water to drink.

Instantly the mother was healed. She sat up in her bed and looked at her villain sons. "I know everything you did," she said. "I have been with you every step of the way, every minute of every day and night."

The magic woman looked at the young woman and nodded, and the young woman took down her harp and played again the song she had played when her third brother would have captured and killed all the animals. The two villains were rolled by the wind to the cursed meadow and placed beside the sleeping brother. All three of them turned to huge granite rocks and they are there to this day, sound asleep and out of the way of decent people.

Everyone for miles around heard the news of the marvels and began to celebrate. The party lasted seven years and seven days with laughter, dancing, singing, and celebration. During that time, the people studied the meaning of all that had happened. Some of them took for themselves the clan of the bear, and vowed never to harm the bear but to be true sisters and brothers. Others made allegiances with the eagle, and promised to do no harm but to be staunch friends. Others took kinship with the otter, others with the salmon, the wolf, and the raven, while the young woman took kinship with both the dog and the horse.

The magic woman stayed for all the days and nights of the celebration, and when the people began to go home again, she stayed on even longer, enjoying the time she spent discussing matters of life and thought with the young woman and her mother.

But the young woman became restless and began to look beyond her front door, beyond her yard, even beyond the meadow where her flocks and herds grazed peacefully. Finally one day she turned to the other two women and said, "There is so much of a world out there, and I have seen but a small corner of it. There are oceans and there are countries, there is magic and there is beauty. I want to travel to see as much of it as I can in my lifetime, but I do not want to leave you all alone."

"How can we be alone," asked her mother, laughing softly, "when we are together?"

"As long as we are together, we are never alone," the magic woman agreed. "Go, and see what it is that you will see. And when you have seen enough, or when you want to come back to visit, whether briefly or longer, you have but to hold your crystal in your hand and, quicker than the wink of your own lovely eye, you will be back here with us again."

The young woman kissed them both. Then, with her silver knife tucked into her boot, with her harp slung over her back, she mounted and rode off on the strong back of the great red mare. The faithful black bitch

68

trotted at her side, and they set out, all three, to see what they would see.

# Four Fables

There was a grey goat had four kids, until the day the grey fox caught them, killed them, and ate them. The goat came home, found her kids dead, and fell into a black sorrow and a red rage. She went out her back door, across the green grass, under the blue sky, until she came to the place where the russet dog was living.

The grey goat jumped on the golden thatch roof under which the russet dog slept and she began pattering around with her little black feet. The puppies in the house, some striped, some speckled, some brown, began to whimper with fear and the russet dog leaped up to protect them, saying

Oh who is that on top of my house
and who is that my deary
who will not leave my kettle to boil
who will not leave my bannock to bake
who frightens my puppies, my dearies?

The grey goat was well aware of the power of rhymes and the force of songs and the magic of music and she tapped her little black feet and answered

There is only me the grey goat, so sad
seeking my poor little kidlings
I mean no harm to your kettle my friend
I mean no harm to your bannock my friend
I mean no harm to your babies.
  The russet dog heard the little bit of a chant and
knew immediately something extraordinary was hap-
pening.
By the earth beneath my feet
By the air above my head
By the sun up in the sky
I have no news of your kidlings.
  The grey goat wept and her tears fell like rain,
but she chanted anyway
My kidlings were the earth to me
my kidlings were the air I breathe
my kidlings were the sun in my sky
but the fox has eaten them all, them all,
the fox has eaten them all.
  The russet dog looked at his own puppies and
thought of how he would feel if they were to be eaten
and he answered
By the blackthorn and the briar
by the earth beneath my feet
by the sun that has gone west
I will rid us of the fox, the fox,
I will rid us of the fox.
  And the russet dog left his puppies in the care of
the grey goat, and went out with his nose to the
ground. He caught the scent of the fox and chased him,
and if he hasn't caught him, he chases him yet.

The fox was fleeing the dog, and had given him the slip
in the rain, but was so hungry his very innards ached.
He went to a farm, sneaked into the shed, and grabbed
the red rooster in his mouth. The rooster squawked,

the farm dog began to bark, the farmer's wife came out of the house with a broom in one hand and a great axe for chopping wood in the other and she set off after the fox who had the rooster in his mouth.

"What a bunch of fools they are!" the rooster said. "They will never catch you, no matter how hard they chase, for you are the fastest in all the world, save one, and the smartest in all the world, save one."

The fox considers himself to be the smartest creature in the world. He growled when he heard what the rooster had to say but the rooster just kept on talking. "The woman can chase and the woman can run, she can wave her broom or drop it, she can holler and shout but she won't catch you, for you are the fastest in the world save one, the smartest in the world. Save one."

The fox yelled, "Who is there faster and smarter than me?" And to yell he had to open his mouth, and when he opened his mouth the rooster flew out and into a tree and yelled "ME, you fool, ME!"

The fox had to flee for his life for the woman was there with her broom and her axe, and she took the rooster home and put him back in the shed and the fox went hungry again.

Banba was sitting at the foot of a tree one day, taking her rest and eating fresh bread with blackberry jam, when she heard a conversation between a crow and her young one.

The mother said, "If you see a human coming with a slender stick in his hand, one end broader than the other, then you must fly away immediately, for it is not a stick, but a gun. Now if you see someone coming toward you and he stops and picks up a rock, fly away immediately for he intends to throw the rock and kill you. But if you see someone coming and he has no stick, and no gun, and does not stop to pick up a rock, you can stay where you are."

"What if he has rocks in his pocket?" the young crow asked.

"Oh my darling!" the mother crow thrilled. "You need no more instruction!"

The fox and the crow were both early risers. One day the fox said he wakened earlier in the morning than the crow did. The crow said he did not.

Do so said the fox
do not said the crow
do so said the fox
do not said the crow
do so said the fox
do not said the crow
betcha said the fox
betcha said the crow

So they made a bet. That evening the crow went to the top of a tree and the fox curled up at the bottom of the tree. The crow went to sleep. The fox cheated and stayed awake, watching the east and waiting for the dawn.

As soon as he saw the very first hint of dawn the fox yelled, "daylight, daylight, daylight," and the crow wakened. Instead of arguing or yawning or accusing the fox of cheating the crow said, "and has been for ten minutes, and has been for ten minutes." The fox thought the crow could see farther from the top of the tree than he could from the bottom, and he lost the bet and the crow won.

Not so far away we could not visit, not so long ago we cannot remember, there was a white-fleeced ewe who had for years willingly given of her wool, and who had every lambing time given birth to twins. It happened this old ewe was grazing near the farmhouse one day and overheard the people discussing what they were going to do in the way of work in the coming weeks.

"Well," said the farmer, "I am going to dispose of that old ewe. She has gone barren, and her fleece is no longer as full and thick as it was. She'll be as tough as an old boot, but tasty."

The ewe could hardly believe what she was hearing. All those years of giving, all those years of being sheared, and now they were going to put her in a stew pot.

She went away from the house so burdened with sadness and grief she could barely hold up her old head.

"Hello, old ewe, why are you so sad?" asked the cow.

"They are going to kill me and eat me," the ewe replied.

"What?" The cow stamped her foot. "I'll go talk to them," she promised.

The cow headed over to the house to let them know what she thought of the dreadful idea.

"Hello, ewe," said the faithful old dog. "Why are you so sad?"

"They're going to kill me and eat me," the ewe said.

"What? Not if I have any say in it," the old dog growled, and she headed for the house to let them know her opinion.

"Hey, old ewe," the cat purred. "Cheer up."

"How can I? They are going to kill me and eat me."

"If they do," the cat vowed, "they'll catch their own mice!"

"Wait for me," said the hen. "They'll be laying their own eggs if they do this."

"I'll go as well," said the old grey goose. "They'll stuff their pillows with grass and straw if they try killing the ewe!"

The cow, the dog, the cat, the hen and the goose headed for the house together, reassuring each other that there is strength in numbers. But before they had a chance to express their opinions, they heard the farmer speaking further about his plans.

"If we're going to be rid of that old ewe," he said, "we might as well get rid of all the worn-out beasts. The cow should be killed and eaten, and we'll get a young one who will give a proper amount of milk. The dog is so old she's half deaf so what use is she as a guard dog? She doesn't have pups any more, and we could always kill her, bury her in the garden, and get some use out of her as fertilizer. The hen hardly ever lays eggs any more, she'd make a good soup, and the goose, well, at least we'd get plenty of goose grease from her. Might as well do them all, they're all too old and should be replaced by younger."

The animals looked at each other, then looked over their shoulders at the old ewe. Then they looked at each other again and walked purposefully away from the house where the plans were being made.

"Ewe, we're on our way. This is not the only life, this is not the only home, and if we are to lose our lives, let us at least not give them away voluntarily."

The ewe straightened her sad self and joined her friends. One foot in front of the other, purposefully and proudly, with dignity and determination, the lot of them went out on their own.

They walked until night came upon them, then moved off the road into a small clearing in a bit of woods, where they passed the night uncomfortable and hungry. In the morning they moved on. Cow, goose, hen, and ewe could eat grass, but poor cat and dog were beginning to feel desperate. When they stopped at a stream to drink their fill, goose went swimming and, despite her age, managed to grab a fish by its tail and flip it on the bank. While cat and dog shared the first fish, goose tried for and got another.

The second night, as darkness began to fall, they spied a light coming from a house. Though it was still a distance away, and though they were all very tired, they moved toward the light.

Close to the house they heard loud drunken voices, which warned them they were not in the presence of honest people. Cat, being the quietest, crept close and peeked through the window. A band of scruffy ne'er-do-wells was gathered together, drinking bad liquor and dividing a pile of stolen gold. The cat listened in horror as the brigands bragged to each other about their thefts, and planned more robberies. Hair on end, the cat hurried back to the others and told them what she had seen and heard.

"We must stop them," the friends decided.

"If we gather together under the window," the old ewe suggested, "and put our heads together, we can each of us call our own call as loudly as possible. I will baa and cow will moo, hen will cackle and cat will wail, dog will bark and even howl, and the dear goose can honk and hiss. It should," she grinned, "make a most dreadful and terrifying cacophony."

No sooner said than done. The friends gathered under the window, put their heads together, took several deep breaths, and cut loose. BAAMOOCAC-WAILBARKOWLHONKHISS! The noise was dreadful enough to stop clocks, curdle milk, scare small children and large men, or turn the course of known history.

Inside the house the brigands froze. One of them, perhaps more clever than the others, perhaps more frightened, leapt up and snuffed out the candle. "If it's the law," he gasped, "they might not see us."

BAAMOOCACWAILBARKOWLHONKHISS! The friends cut loose again. And in the darkness the vile noise seemed louder and more fierce than ever. The villains tumbled over each other, scurrying for the door. In their terror and haste, they left behind the gold they had been so busy dividing.

The friends watched as the thieves pelted off into the dark night, then they walked into the house. In no time at all, the money was back in one pile, the pile safe in the hands of the friends.

In the bush, the villains waited, but no armed patrol of police raided the house, no regiment of soldiers arrived, and no group of angry townspeople came to retrieve the money. The villains began to wonder why it was they had run.

"Where will you sleep tonight, friend cow?" asked the old ewe.

"I will sleep behind the door, where I have always slept," said the cow. "And you?"

"I will sleep in the middle of the floor, where I always do."

"I," said the hen, "will roost up in the rafters, as I always do."

"And I," said the dog, "will sleep in front of the fire."

"I think," said the cat, "that I will sleep on the counter, near that pile of candles."

"And I," said the goose, "don't want to sleep in the house at all. I'll sleep outside, under a rose bush, as I have always done."

The good friends kissed each other goodnight, and each went to her chosen place to pass a comfortable night.

No sooner were they settled down to rest than one of the villains crept up to the house and peeked through the window, trying to see what in all holiness had made such an abominable racket. He looked and looked but there is never much to be seen in the darkness. He listened, but heard no sound of threat. With his heart in his throat, he tiptoed to the door, opened it, and went inside.

The thief moved to where he thought there was a pile of candles on the counter, but as he reached for the candles the old cat dug all her claws into his hand. Five claws on each foot, four feet to the cat, twenty small daggers ripping and gouging. The thief screeched, dropped the candle, then stepped on it and lost his balance. He fell to the floor and the dog was on him, snapping and growling, biting and bouncing. The thief leapt up and ran as fast as he could, but the old ewe put down her head and slammed him in the belly, knocking him jack-knifed across the room. The cow fired a sideways kick or two, the old hen was on his head digging and spurring with her feet, and when he finally made it through the door to the yard, the goose flew between his legs, slamming him on the shins with her powerful wings.

Yelling and yodelling, hollering and screeching, the thief broke free and raced away with his companions following him. Miles away, out of breath entirely, the hysterical thieves dropped together in a pile beside the road.

"What was all that about?" asked one.

"I went to get a candle," said the cowardly one, "and a soldier was at me with his sword, stab stab slash slash. When I tried to defend myself, a big black policeman was all over me, punching and biting. When I managed to get away from him, two others were on me, the grey-haired one giving judo kicks to my belly and the brown-haired one striking from behind. And when I got away from them and got to the door, a cheeky little karate expert was all over my head, hammering on me. I got out the door and was running for my life when a professional wrestler got me by the legs and it is only by absolute mercy I got away. There must have been," he finished, "at least twenty-five armed soldiers hidden inside that house."

That was all the villains had to hear. Tired as they were, they were on their feet and running away again, for the wicked always flee when nobody chases them.

Back at the house the ewe, the cow, the hen, the cat, and dog, and the goose settled in with the gold. There was enough of it for them to live comfortably all the days of their lives.

# THE CHARNEL ROOM

The Scaldies are not travelling people. They prefer to stay in one spot, living on their little bit of land, learning its every way, making it spouse, parent, and child to them and their families, sometimes even burying their bones on the land, that they might become part of it.

Now it happened there was a Scaldie widow with two daughters and all she had to feed them was a garden, and in the garden there was only kale and turnips and once in a while some cabbage.

On a particular day a group of travelling people stopped at the widow's farm and asked if they would be allowed to stop their wagons in her field and feed their horses on her grass.

"Yes," the widow said, "and no need to worry about your horses eating all the grass for I have no animals left who will need it. I had a pig but the great grey horse came and took it. I had a goat for milk, but that same great grey horse came and took it, and all my chickens have been taken by ones, by twos and even by threes by that same great grey horse."

"Now that's a strange thing," said one of the young travelling women. "As much as I know about horses, I have never heard of one eating pigs, goats, or hens, nor eggs for that matter, nor milk either. It is a most unusual horse."

"Yes," said the widow, "and the good dog I had who would warn me of the horse's coming vanished the night before the pigs disappeared and I expect the horse took it first."

So the travelling people stayed in the meadow with their horses grazing on the rich grass, and they invited the widow and her daughters to have supper with them.

After supper, when the widow and her daughters went back to the house, the oldest daughter said she was going to take her spinning out to the kale garden.

"That horse is sure to come back," she said, "and eat every speck of kale, leaving us with nothing."

Out she went to set up her spinning wheel. She did not know the travelling woman watched from her cart.

Presently the great grey horse appeared and began to eat the kale. The brave daughter picked up a stick and beat on the horse, yelling, "off with you, ugly beast, off!" But the stick stuck to the horse, the young woman's hand stuck to the stick, and the horse ran off, taking stick and woman with him.

The travelling woman followed, as fast as she could. When the horse reached the great green hill, he called, "open open, oh green hill, open for the son of the king; open open oh green hill, open for the widow's daughter," and the great green hill opened and swallowed the two. There was nothing for the travelling woman but to go back and report what she had seen and heard.

Inside the hill, the great grey horse turned into a man and smiled a charming smile at the widow's daughter. He warmed water for her to wash, he made a soft bed for her to lie down on, and he put bread, cheese, and milk on the table for her to eat. Then he retired to his own bedroom and left her alone all night.

In the morning he handed her the keys to the entire place. "You may open every room in the house," he said, "except for the one with the mark on the door. You must not open that room for any reason. And if you are good, and do as I say, when I return I will reward you."

Off he went and the daughter began unlocking doors, looking for a way out. Each room was more beautiful than the one before, each filled with more treasure than the one before, but not one of them had a door that would lead her outside the great green hill. Finally, there was only one door she had not opened, and it was the one with the mark on it. She opened it even though he had warned her not to do so.

She stepped into the room and was up to her knees in blood. The room was full of dead women. Shaking with horror she backed out of the room, closed the door and locked it. Then she noticed the blood on her legs.

She went to the first room, where the wash water was still in the basin, and she scrubbed the blood away. Then she poured the bloody water down the hole in the floor and thought she would be safe. He would never know she had opened the door.

In the house built in the heart of the great green hill there was a lovely grey and white cat and she went to the young woman and rubbed against her leg and said, "please, please, do you have a little sup of cream for me, please please?"

"Get out of here, you filthy damned beast!" the widow's daughter said, her nerves about to break.

"Give me a dab of cream to drink and I'll lick the last of the blood off your heel," the cat offered.

The young woman looked down and saw that there was blood still on her heel. "Go away," she said. "I can do a better job of it myself," and she wiped at the blood on her heel. The cat shrugged, and went off to lie under the stove, purring her own version of the story to herself.

The king's son came back and smiled at the widow's daughter. "And were you a good woman today?" he asked.

"Yes," she said, handing him the keys.

"Really?" His smile changed. "Then how is it I see blood on your foot?" And he lopped her head off with his sword, and threw her in the charnel room with the other dead women.

The travelling woman had told the others what she had seen and heard. They had searched for the young woman, but found no trace. And that night the second daughter said, "I will go out and guard the kale from the horse or he will eat everything we have," and she took her sewing out with her, to sit outside by the garden and be the guard. "I promise," she soothed her mother, "I will not take up a stick and hit him the way my sister did for I don't want the stick to stick to him and me to stick to the stick."

The horse arrived, and the second daughter tried to scare him away by flapping her sewing in his face. The sewing stuck to the horse, then stuck to the young woman's hand, and she could not let go. The horse raced off with the sewing stuck to him and the young woman stuck to the sewing and the travelling woman racing after to see what she could see.

"Open open great green hill," the horse cried, "open for the son of the king. Open open great green hill, open for the widow's second daughter," and the hill did, and they went in and the hill closed again, leaving the travelling woman outside, again.

Everything went as before. The horse became the king's son, and he warmed water for her to wash, he made her a soft bed, he left bread, he left cheese, he left milk, and he left her alone. And in the morning he gave her the keys and told her she could open any door in the house except the one with the mark on it, and if she was a good woman and left the marked door alone, he would reward her when he returned.

Off he went and she began opening doors, looking for a way out of the place in the heart of the hill. No way out. She opened the marked door, stepped inside the room and was up to her knees in blood. She saw all the dead women, including her own dear sister, and she knew in a flash she was in more trouble than she had thought possible.

She closed the door and locked it, then went back to the first room to clean herself of the blood. The cat came up and said, "please please, a sup of cream for me, please please."

"Oh, go away!" the young woman said. "I hate cats!"

"Please, please, a sup of cream for me and in return I'll lick the blood from your heel."

"I can do a better job of it myself," she said, and she washed her entire foot, then poured the bloody water down the hole in the floor.

The cat went to her place and lay under the stove purring her own version of the story to herself. And the son of the king came back and asked, "Were you a good woman today?"

"I was," she said.

"And did you open the marked door?" he asked.

"I did not," she said.

"Then what is that on your heel?" he asked, and out with his axe and off with her head and she was in the room again, lying right next to her sister and each as dead as the other.

That night it was the travelling woman who guarded the kale. The great grey horse arrived, the travelling woman rushed it, and hit it with her hand. Her hand stuck to the horse and off they went, racing through the night.

"Open open great green hill," the horse called, "open for the son of the king. Open open great green hill, open for the widow's daughter," and the hill opened and they were inside.

He was no longer a horse, but the son of the king and he gave her hot water as he had done before, and gave her a soft bed, left her bread, left her cheese, left her milk, and left her alone.

In the morning he handed her the keys and told her about the doors and off he went. And the travelling woman began unlocking the doors, looking for a way out. Each room was more lovely than the one before, each room filled with more treasure than the one before, but none of them was a way out.

So she opened the marked door, stepped inside, and was up to her knees in blood. She saw the dead women, including the widow's two daughters, and she thought sure she would be sick before she got herself out of this mess. She hurried out of the charnel room, went to the first room and began to wash the blood from her feet and legs.

"A small sup of milk," the cat pleaded, "just a small sup. I haven't had a drop in three days and if you will give me some milk, I will clean that mess off your heel."

"Oh, you poor wee thing," the travelling woman said, "you're as bad off as myself," and she gave the cat the milk the king's son had left for her. The cat drank it all and said some words even the travelling woman didn't understand, although the travelling people have a language of their own and can speak the languages of many other people as well.

The son of the king came home and looked at the travelling woman and asked, "Were you a good woman today"

"Yes," she said, "I was indeed."

"Did you open the marked door?" he asked.

"And was it not yourself told me not to do that?" she answered quickly. "And would I not be a fool to disobey someone who can give orders to the very hills?"

He checked her heels and found not a sign of blood. "Good," he said, "you did as you were told. Well, and if you continue this way your reward will be that I will marry you."

"Do me no favours," the travelling woman said in the language of the cat and the cat laughed but the son of the king understood nothing.

He went to bed and left her bread, left her milk, left her cheese, and left her alone. She shared the bread, milk, and cheese with the cat, who slept with her that night on the soft bed.

In the morning, off went the son of the king to do whatever it was he did during his days and the cat told the woman, "When he comes back he will ask you what gift you wish him to send to your mother as a token of his marriage to you."

"I'm not who he thinks I am," the travelling woman said. And she told the cat the story.

The cat shrugged. "What difference?" she said. "He'll ask anyway, and you tell him that there are ever so many big chests in this place and your poor mother without so much as one. Tell him you have cleaned three of the chests and that you want him to give them to your mother."

"But what—"

"Do as I say," the cat yawned, "or stay here and marry him and the day after your wedding you'll be in that room with the others."

86

So the travelling woman busied herself sorting and cleaning the rooms of treasure, cleaning up and tidying up and washing three huge travel chests. And when the son of the king came home and saw how much tidier his treasure was, he said, "You are a good woman, indeed. Tell me what I can give to your mother as a token of our marriage."

"See those chests?" the young woman said. "Well, you have thousands of them and my mother has nothing like that at all. If you would be so kind as to give her these, I would be very grateful."

"Is that all?" he laughed. "I thought you would ask for gold and silver and jewels."

"No," she said, "just the chests."

"I'll take them after I return tomorrow," he promised. And he left her bread, he left her cheese, he left her milk, and he left her alone. In the morning, off he went to do whatever it was he did when he was gone.

"Now," said the cat, "see that club on the wall? Take it and go into the charnel room and bash the widow's daughters on the head. Hard."

"Yuck," said the young woman, but she took the club and went into the room and she swung the club and she bashed each of them on the head. And they stood up—whole, hale, and hearty.

"Into the chests," the cat said. And the young women, remembering what had happened when they had ignored the cat, climbed into two of the chests. "Now," the cat lectured, "if at any time the lid of the chest begins to lift you are to call, 'I see you, I see you,' and that's all you have to do," and she closed the lids. "You," she said to the travelling woman, "are to convince the king's son that you have eyes like a hawk and will see him if he stops on his voyage or peeks in the chests."

"Well, all right," said the young woman, "but it makes no sense to me."

He came home and she asked him if he remembered what he had said about presenting the chests to her mother. He said he did and she said, "you had better take them one at a time, they're very heavy."

"I can take two at a time," he bragged. "I am stronger than you would believe."

"You'll never make it," she said. "You'll have to put them down and rest."

"No," he said, his vanity stung.

"I'll know if you do," she laughed, "I have eyes like a hawk and I'll see you if you put them down before you get there, and if you do, I'll say I told you so."

Off he went, one chest under each arm, and as soon as he was out of the great green hill he was a horse again, with the chests on his back. He ran right to the widow's house and put the chests on her steps. Then off he raced again to pick up the third chest. When he had gone to deliver it, the travelling woman picked up the cat, tucked it under her arm, and said, "great green hill, great green hill, he told you to open for the widow's daughter, and you did, and I entered. But he lied, he lied, he lied, he lied, I am not the widow's daughter at all," and the hill roiled with anger and cast the travelling woman and the cat from its centre. They flew through the air and landed in the kale garden, then the travelling woman raced into the house before the great grey horse arrived with the third chest.

The widow was weeping with joy over the safe return of her daughters, and she would have given a heartfull of thanks to the travelling woman. But the travelling woman told them all to hush and be still, the great grey horse was coming. "Feed the cat," she told the two young daughters, and they were in such a hurry to atone for their previous disgrace they almost fell over themselves and each other in their haste to find food for the cat.

The great grey horse galloped up and put the third chest on the steps, then headed off for the great green hill. The travelling woman opened the door, grabbed the chest, hauled it inside, and opened it up to reveal a wealth of treasure, so much that if none of them did another lick of work from one day to the next to the end of time, they would still be wealthy.

"There is nothing to eat here," the cat said sadly.

"Eat a mouse," one daughter snapped, "heaven knows we have enough of them!"

"No," said the cat, "if I eat the mouse the dog will chase me, if the dog chases me the goat will chase the dog, if the goat chases the dog the cow will chase the goat, if the cow chases the goat the farmer will chase the cow and all because I chased the mouse," and the cat left, still looking for something to eat.

"Would you share in the treasure?" the widow asked.

"All I would want would be enough to buy a lovely silver flute," the travelling woman said, and she took two pink pearls, tucked them in her pocket, said goodbye and left to catch up to her people.

Half a mile down the road she passed the cat and offered it a ride on her shoulder.

Meanwhile, the great grey horse had reached the great green hill. "Oh great green hill," he called, "open for the son of the king."

"You lied," the hill growled, and it refused to open for him. The great grey horse was in a fury. He turned and saw the young travelling woman walking down the road with the cat on her shoulder and he went at her, intending to trample her into the ground. But she was a travelling woman who knew the secret shared by the horses, and because he was in his guise as a horse he had to honour the ancient pact. She led him to the next village and traded him to a rich man for enough money to buy a beautiful silver flute, a wonderful burnished harp, and a fine healthy goat to provide milk for the cat. And she still had her two pink pearls with her.

And I know it is true because it was that very cat told me the story.

# THE TOWERS

It happened that there was a knight known far and wide as a fair and honest man who never oppressed his people. He had three daughters who were as lovely as any could be, and one had blonde hair, one had black hair, and the third had copper hair.

One day the three daughters were walking along the beach at the foot of the great cliff on which sat their father's castle, and up from the waves rose an enormous beastie, all covered with barnacles, dripping slime, with long strands of seaweed dangling from her dreadful horned head.

The knight grabbed his sword and began the long run down the path from the top of the cliff to the beach, but before he was halfway down the beastie scooped up all three daughters and like that, they were gone, drawn under the water and taken off to nobody knew where for reasons nobody would dare contemplate.

The knight grieved and sorrowed, and nothing anyone did could wipe the tears from his eyes nor mend the great rift in his heart. He stopped knighting and sat brooding, his war horse going to fat and a fine rust forming on his armour and his blade.

Thirteen months passed and then it happened that Banba decided to take herself out in a small boat to do some fishing. Two young men asked if they could go with her for they, too, were drawn to the idea of a fine meal of flaky baked fish. Since they were travelling people and used to being in boats, Banba agreed, and off they went to drop their lines.

They pushed the small boat from the shore to the sea and jumped in, with only a waterskin and a piece of cheese for lunch, and they all remarked to each other what a lovely sunny day they had for their fun.

No sooner were they in the boat, floating free of the beach, than a huge wind came from nowhere and grabbed them. Nothing they did made any difference. They pulled on the oars to no avail, they tried to set a sail and tack back to no avail, they dropped an anchor and it did not grab anything. The boat went where the wind wished.

"Well," said Banba, settling herself as comfortably as she could, "it's out of our hands. Nothing happens for no reason, and it's foolish to try to fight your wyrd."

The young travelling men were not happy to hear talk of wyrds, which are fates, but they knew Banba's words were true. They, too, settled themselves as best they could, and vowed they would very carefully ration their bit of food and water.

Seven days and seven nights they were pushed by that wind. And though they sipped the water, the skin was never empty; though they nibbled sparingly on the cheese, they did not finish it; and though they were both hungry and thirsty, they were not in any danger.

As quickly as it had come up, the wind died, depositing them on a wide white sandy beach.

"My stars," said one of the young men, "and where are we now?"

An otter poked her head from the water and said, "This is where the daughters of the knight have been taken. They are going to marry three giants who live at the top of that rock face."

"And do they want to marry these giants, then?" asked the second young travelling man.

"No. But giants do as giants do and giants do not think the wishes of others matter. The young women will be married whether they want to be or not."

"It must be stopped," said the one young man.

"How would a body get up that cliff?" asked the second young man.

"Nobody ever has," said the otter, and she went back under the waves.

The first young man studied the face of the cliff and noticed a crack angling up toward the top. He started climbing up the crack, determined to stop these unwelcome marriages. He was halfway up the cliff when an enormous raven came at him, tearing at his face with her talons, ripping at his flesh with her beak. The young man was forced back down the cliff, inch by inch, foot by foot, until he was back on the wide white sandy beach, his head and face torn and bleeding.

The second young man grabbed a stick and headed right up the crack down which his brother had come. When he was halfway up the same raven came at him the same way and though he flailed with his stick, though he threw rocks and curses, though he struggled bravely to defend himself, still the raven ripped and tore and slashed and the young man was forced to retreat.

At last Banba herself went to the crack and started climbing up carefully, placing her hands where the others had placed theirs, placing her feet where the others had placed theirs. When she was halfway up the crack the same raven came back and started ripping and tearing at her face.

"Bugger off," Banba laughed, "you can rip and I will heal, you can rend and I will heal, you can tear and claw and do as you will, you will not scar me nor deter me nor keep me from doing what I have set out to do and furthermore, you are a frowzy, blowzy, bedraggled, and very ugly bird whose mother ought to have laid her eggs in the mouth of a fox and saved the world the bother of putting up with you."

"Why you evil-mouthed thing," the raven screeched, "I am lovely! My feathers are not bedraggled, they are bright and shiny and well cared for. I am sleek and well fed, I am beautiful." And the raven went on arguing and praising her own loveliness and the whole time Banba just kept climbing up the crack until she was at the top of the cliff.

"See," the raven pouted, "and I even let you climb where nobody has climbed before. You should give me something."

"Give you something," Banba laughed. "A slap on the side of the head is about all I'll give you!"

"You'll be sorry," the raven warned. "I will go and warn my master the giant and before much longer you'll be sitting next to the knight's daughter and you'll be weeping and crying the same as her."

"Oh, what a lie," Banba laughed. "There is no giant, there is no castle, and there is certainly no such thing as a princess weeping as if her heart would break."

"You think not!" The raven went into a fit of rage. "Well, you'll see if I'm telling the truth or not," and she grabbed Banba by the shirt and flew with her over the mountains and over the trees, over the rivers and over the streams to the window of a tower and into a room where a blonde young woman sat weeping bitter tears.

"Well," said Banba, "you were right and I was wrong and I apologize most sincerely."

"So you should," said the raven, still sulking.

"And you," Banba asked the young woman, "why are you crying?"

"I am to be married to the giant tomorrow and it will be my death."

"Why will it be your death?"

"Well think about it, you silly old thing," the young woman snapped. "I am a mortal woman of mortal size and he is a giant. He has had a dozen wives and each of them died on her wedding night."

"Then what are you doing sitting here crying? Why aren't you saving yourself?"

"How can I? There is no way out but the window and if you just look out of it you'll see it's a long drop down. And were I to survive, I don't know where I am so how do I know how to get away? And if I did, how would I pass the open sea? And if I did, what would I eat?"

"Well." Banba shook her head with disgust. "You KNOW you're going to die tomorrow night anyway, so what's better about dying in the marriage bed of a giant than dying of a quick broken neck from jumping out the window? If you don't know where you are, you at least know what is going to happen, so why sit on your lovely backside like a lump of tallow? If you did get to the open sea, wouldn't it be better to drown clean than die the death that awaits you? And why worry about whether or not you'll have something to eat? Once he holds you and hugs you and kills you I can guarantee you won't taste food again. You may be the most beautiful daughter but you are a pudding," Banba concluded, and she cursed some hearty curses, jumped out the window and headed away from the tower.

The raven flew up and grabbed her by the shirt. In a zip she had flown Banba to a second tower, and taken her in through the window to where a dark-haired young woman sat weeping helplessly.

Well, it was the same thing. "What good would it do, there is no way out but the window and I don't know where I am and what about the ocean and what would I eat and what would I drink and anyway . . ."

"You KNOW you're going to die," Banba yelled. "You KNOW what he's going to do. Better to jump out the window, break your neck, and thwart his plans than to just sit here crying. You might be beautiful but you are as big a pudding as your sister." And she jumped out the window and was walking away when the raven grabbed her by the shirt and hauled her up in the air, then flew her off to a third tower.

In this tower things were different. The copper-haired daughter was chained to the wall, with a big ball attached to a chain and the chain attached to a metal strap and the metal strap fastened around her ankle. She had bruises all over her body, scratches on her arms, and a very angry gleam in her eye.

"Well," Banba grinned, "and look at you! You don't look much like the daughter of a rich knight."

"If you can't help," the young woman snapped, "don't hinder! If you haven't got something constructive to say, shut your mouth."

"Tsk tsk," Banba laughed again. "And why are you all tied up and chained and scratched and bruised when your sisters are still as lovely as ever, sitting on footstools, weeping?"

She took the jug of wine from the table and offered the young woman a sip, but the young woman shook her head stubbornly. "He's put something in it," she said, "and if I drink it I'll get very sleepy. I made that mistake once, I won't make it again. I'd be unable to do anything and tomorrow night I'd die and not even be aware of how it happened."

"I have a skin of water here," Banba said, "and it has nothing in it but its own pure self. You will not get sleepy, only less thirsty and less weak."

The young woman smiled and drank happily. Banba took a piece of cheese from the table and offered it to the young woman but she refused, saying the same thing. "He put something in it and it will make me sleepy and I won't even wake up when he marries me and kills me."

"But how did you get out of this tower?" Banba asked.

"I ripped up my clothes and I ripped up the curtains and I ripped up the bedding and I made a rope. It didn't go all the way to the bottom but I went down it anyway. And when I got to the end of it, I jumped. I sprained my ankle, but I was out of the tower. And then I ran. Except with a sprained ankle I didn't so much run as hobble and limp."

"In which direction did you run?" Banba asked.

"AWAY, you idiot," the girl snapped.

"But if you didn't know where you were going. . ."

"Oh, but I did," the girl argued. "I was going AWAY."

"With no food or water?"

"I can live for weeks without food, I can live for days without water, but I'll be dead tomorrow night if I just sit here like a pudding!"

"How would you get over the ocean?"

"I'd sit on my fist, lean back against my thumb and turn my bottom lip into a sail, you daft ninny," the girl cursed. "I'd rather drown than die the way I'll die if he marries me."

Banba smiled and Banba danced and Banba capered a happy caper, then she took hold of the raven and shoved its beak in the lock on the chain. "A choice," she said, "open the lock or I'll break your beak."

"Traitor," said the raven bitterly, but she opened the

lock, and the chains holding the young woman to the wall were released.

Banba then shoved the raven's foot into the lock that held the ball and chain to the young woman's ankle. "Open the lock or I'll break your foot," she said, and the raven cawed bitterly, but twisted her talon like a key and opened the lock.

"Now," Banba ordered, "take us both to the seashore or I will pull all the feathers off your body and leave you naked for others to laugh at."

The raven was furious, but she did as Banba told her and flew back to the seashore with the two of them.

"You're free," Banba said, "and I promise to tell everyone how you helped me. I will not," she said craftily, "tell them that I tricked you, for they would laugh at you. I will tell them you were brave and noble and a true-hearted friend."

The young woman rested on the beach for a moment, then started up the crack in the cliff. "Where are you going?" Banba asked.

"My sisters are still prisoners," the young woman said, "and I cannot just leave them to a certain death."

"They are puddings who will not help themselves," Banba argued.

"They are my sisters," the girl said, "and I cannot be free if I know they are prisoners, I cannot be happy if I know I left them to die."

She continued up the crack. Halfway up the raven flew at her but Banba put herself between the girl and the bird, and the raven had too much good sense to try to defeat the white-haired woman with the perfumed breath. She sighed, and looked at Banba, shrugged her shoulders, and said something very similar to Here We Go Again. She grabbed the young woman's shirt with one foot and Banba's shirt with the other foot and flew them over hill and over dale, over mountain and over forest, over river and over stream to the room in the tower where the dark-haired young woman still sat crying.

"For heaven's sake," the youngest sister said, "get up off your backside and DO something about your situation."

"What can I do?" the sister mourned.

"JUMP," the red-haired one said, but the other wept.

So the younger sister tore her sister's clothes into strips and tore the curtains into strips and tore the bedding into strips. She made a rope and put it out the window and managed to talk her sister into climbing down, although the talking took much longer than the making of the rope.

The dark-haired sister was halfway down the rope when who should show up but the giant.

"Ho my lovely," he said, "do you think you can escape from me?" and he reached out to grab her.

The youngest sister, still in the tower, saw and heard everything. She grabbed the chamber pot from under the bed and heaved it with all her might.

Down it slammed onto the head of the giant, settling over his skull down to his top lip, covering his eyes so he was blind. He roared and shouted, he bellowed and screamed, he stumbled around trying to get the chamber pot off his head, but he tripped over a rock he could not see and he fell, striking his head on a bigger rock and knocking himself senseless.

The dark-haired sister was so terrified she screeched twice, let go of the rope, and fell to the ground, where the giant's enormous belly cushioned her fall so she was not hurt.

The dark-haired sister jumped from the tower and she, too, landed on the giant's belly. Or near it, anyway, causing him such pain he wakened and screamed. He jumped up, the chamber pot still on his head and, stumbling and roaring, he raced off across his own field and ran right into an enormous oak tree. The tree had been waiting seven thousand years for this chance and it dropped a branch right on top of the giant's head. That was the last anyone ever heard of that giant.

Banba jumped next, and of course could not be killed or even hurt. There were now too many of them for the poor raven to carry, so they went to the giant's stable and soon the three of them were riding off on wonderful horses, the raven sitting on Banba's shoulder, as proud as a raven can be.

"The giant's castle is full of treasure," the dark-haired sister said. "We should take it all and give it to our father."

"And leave our sister to die, I suppose," the youngest sister yelled.

"Why are you always yelling at me?" the dark-haired sister wept.

"Because you are so absolutely unbearably stupid," the youngest one said honestly. "No thank yous, I notice. No oh my goodness I hope you aren't hurt. No thank you for coming. Just why don't we grab some treasure and take weeks to get it home after which we'll give it to someone who already has more of it than he can keep track of and in the meantime someone dies. You really are just too stupid for words."

Banba sighed and closed her ears because she hated bickering and nitpicking and yapping to no avail, and she knew nothing the youngest daughter said, however true it might be, would change the dark-haired sister who would always regret not having scooped the treasure.

The wonderful horses took them to the tower where the blonde-haired sister sat weeping and wailing and howling and moaning. The raven carried them up one at a time.

"Come ON!" the red-haired youngest said.

"But what about—" the blonde-haired sister began her litany.

"I did it, my dear," the dark one gushed, "and now I am safe and you can do it, too, I'm sure. And maybe the raven will carry us down so we won't have to jump or climb."

"No," the raven said, "you surely to heaven ought to be willing to do SOMETHING yourself, otherwise why should I bother?"

"Grab her," the dark-haired sister said to Banba, "and twist her neck and make her do it."

"No," Banba said, "you really do have to do something for yourself. The raven has already put herself at risk for you, why should she risk more for your freedom than you're willing to risk?"

The debate might have gone on for much longer but just then the door burst open and in came the giant, who was even more enormous than the other one.

"Ho ho," he chortled. "Not just one lovely bride but four." And he rushed toward them to scoop them all up in his hands.

The youngest sister hit the floor and rolled toward the giant. She grabbed his shoelaces and tied them together, then continued rolling toward the far wall. The giant lunged at her but his shoelaces pulled him up short. He fell forward and slammed his head on the edge of the bed, knocking himself unconscious.

"Out the door," Banba yelled, and the blonde-haired sister and the dark-haired sister did as they were told. "Raven, save yourself," Banba called, and the raven went out the window. "Come ON," the red-haired sister said, grabbing Banba by the hand and heading for the door.

They slammed it shut and locked the big locks—one, two, three, four locks—then down the stairs they went.

"My," said the blonde sister, "look at all the treasure."

"Never mind the cursed treasure," the red-haired sister said. "It weighs tons and tons and tons and we haven't got the time!"

Out of the castle they raced, and over to the stables they ran, and when Banba whispered to the horses the secret they shared, all of the horses very willingly left the giant's stables.

"Look at the lovely saddles," the blonde-haired sister said, "all gold and jewels and silver."

"And weighing tons and tons," the youngest sister said. "Have some consideration for the poor horses, you fool."

The horses very happily raced off carrying the four women, and though it was a long and difficult journey, they did not mind one little bit because without the saddles their lives were made much more pleasant.

At this moment the third giant, the one who had thought to marry the youngest daughter, came home to his castle and, of course, found her gone. He went to his stables and got his horses and put on their saddles and headed off thinking the second giant had come and stolen the red-haired sister. He bellowed with rage and promised to avenge the imagined insult. The noise he made cracked the branches on the trees in the mighty oak forest. The force of his breath blew the broken branches through the air and they flew into the ocean. There they tangled themselves into a huge platform at the foot of the enormous cliff.

The third giant kept roaring and yelling and howling and shouting until he found the body of the giant he thought had wronged him. "It's that first one," he decided, "came and killed this one and stole my princess and thinks he will have a fine time tomorrow night marrying all three of them." And he whipped his poor horses until the blood ran down their flanks, and continued on to the castle of the first giant.

Banba and the women reached the top of the cliff and dismounted. "You are free now," Banba told the horses, and she headed for the crack to climb down to the bottom.

"I know a quicker way," the raven said. "Tie the tail of one horse to the mane of another, then tie the tail of that one to the mane of a third, and the tail of the third to the mane of a fourth, and on and on, and then the first one can be lowered slowly to the beach, and each after that, and the last ones can climb down on the pyramid made by the first ones."

It was done quicker than it was described. And the women climbed down the pyramid of wonderful horses, and soon they were all on the beach where the two beaten and ripped and slashed and bruised and badly damaged young men were waiting.

"Well," the men said, "all these branches came flying through the air and fell into the water and tangled into this great raft. We thought of getting on it and going home but we didn't want to leave without you."

Banba and the women got onto the raft, then the young men limped onto the raft, then Banba looked at the horses who had helped them. "You can come or you can stay," she said.

"We'd rather go than stay," the horses decided, "because if those big Fomors find us it's back to the stables and those heavy saddles for us," and they climbed one by one onto the raft.

By now the third giant had arrived at the castle of the first giant. He dismounted and stormed into the castle roaring with rage and swinging his huge sword. The horses looked at each other, then sniffed at the ground, and the whole story was revealed to them by the grasses and flowers. Off they went, desperation giving them speed, to join the other horses.

The giant went up the castle stairs to the room at the top of the tower. He hammered and banged and slammed away at the first lock until it broke, then he started on the second lock, and all this noise wakened the first giant, who decided he was under attack. He grabbed up his sword and started smashing at his own door from the inside while the third giant smashed at the door from the outside and both of them howled curses and challenges.

The last of the horses was arranging herself on the raft when the desperate saddled fugitives arrived at the top of the cliff.

"Help," they called, and one would have thrown herself off the cliff and taken her chances, but the others neighed they should tie the tail of the first to the mane of the second and the tail of the second to the mane of the third and so on, and lower themselves to the beach. Which they did, and then they untied each other and swam out to the raft. And the sound of the battle came to them on the wind, the cursing and yelling, the howling and insulting, the roaring and bravery and glory of it all.

There is only so much a door can stand. The one separating the giants gave up. It turned itself into splinters and slivers and suddenly the two giants were face to face with each other. They were both so ugly that each one scared the liver and lights out of the other. One ran out the front door screaming and one ran out the back door screaming and for all anyone knows they are still running from each other screaming with horror.

The wind sprang up and caught hold of the raft, the raven came down and settled on Banba's shoulder, and all of them were transported across the surface of the sea.

Seven days and seven nights the wind blew and then

the raft was washed up on the beach not far from the home of the knight who was father to the young women. He came racing from his castle, weeping with joy, and the blonde-haired daughter ran toward him happily, followed by the dark-haired daughter and, finally, the re- haired daughter.

"Come with us," she said, "I'm sure he'll throw a party. And I'm sure he'll reward you."

"Oh, a party is it," the young travelling men said. "Who could resist a party?"

"A party indeed," Banba decided and she followed them with the horses following her and the raven riding on her shoulder.

A party it was. For a year and a day they partied and sang, they danced and they ate, they laughed and repeated again and again the story of their adventure.

"You could marry my daughter," the knight offered one young man, "and live here in the castle, with all your needs met for all your life."

"Ah, but my needs are met, kind sir," the young man said, "and I don't want to marry a woman simply because her father thinks it a good idea. There's a young travelling woman I've known for some time and it is she thinks it's a good idea we should marry. I'd sooner do that and be welcome than this other and be merely tolerated."

"Well," said the father to the second, "would you like to marry one of my daughters and live here for your entire life, taken care of and your every need met?"

"Oh, my every need is met," the young man said, "although I do thank you for the offer."

"And you?" the knight asked Banba.

"Are you inviting me to marry one of your daughters?" she laughed. The knight glared at her and said nothing. Banba laughed again. "I've everything I need," she said, "and I suspect the party is winding down so I

105

think I'll be on my way. A good day to you good knight," and she left, waving her thanks and whistling to let the horses know she was leaving.

She and the young men were no more than a few minutes away from the castle when they heard a voice calling "Hey, wait for me!" and the youngest daughter, the red-haired one, came pelting toward them, her hair shining in the sunlight. "I'm coming, too," she said.

"You don't want to stay in the castle and marry a prince and have all your needs met?"

"If I stay in the castle and marry a prince, believe me, few of my needs will be met," and she laughed and winked, and slung her harp over her shoulder, then vaulted onto one of the horses and set her face toward the distance.

Banba whispered something to the raven sitting on her shoulder and the raven nodded and Banba taught the travelling men and the errant daughter the secret she shared with the horses, and since that very day the travelling people have been the ones to gentle and train the finest of horses. As for the red-haired daughter, well, she played the harp and she played the lute, she played the fiddle and she played the bodhran and she never married but her every need was met, and if she hasn't died of a happy old age she is out there still going where she wishes to go, doing what she wishes to do, seeing what she wishes to see, meeting the needs of others, and living the life she lives.

# THE ABERSGAIC

There was a woman went to a great May Day celebration and while dancing and singing, drinking and laughing, she met a young soldier and made a fool of herself. The soldier went back to his regiment and the young woman was left with only the proof of her foolishness, which grew and grew until the whole world knew and at last she had a daughter.

Life was hard for them both, nothing but work and more work to keep them barely alive. Then a bishop came riding up and asked, "Are you the one made a fool of herself with a young soldier some eighteen years ago?"

"Oh, yes, it is me was a fool and I've paid for my sin, and every day the price is higher and every day I pay some more," she said, although she did not feel the least bit sorry for herself, she'd done it and what good to regret what was passed.

"Well," said the bishop, "the soldier made a hero of himself and died in the doing of it and he's left a letter saying you are to have his abersgaic." So saying he

107

handed her a haversack, and off he rode to collect his dues.

The woman had no more use for the abersgaic than any of us would have so she gave it to her daughter as a keepsake of her father. The daughter had little use of it either, until the day came she was to go to the fair in the next county to deliver the puppies which had come of their good bitch. She put the puppies in the abersgaic and put it on her back with the puppies' heads poking out, and off she went to the fair.

At the fair, people saw the heads of the fine puppies poking out of the abersgaic and they asked her, "Why do you carry those puppies instead of letting them walk?"

"Well," she said, "and why should they walk all the way to the fair and then walk home again? They are fine puppies and will grow into fine bitches and every one of them trained to a fare-thee-well, and trained by me myself." She lifted the puppies from the abersgaic and said, "Now, my fine puppies, show what you can do," and they moved to the signs she made with her hands. They rounded up sheep and moved them from pen to pen, they jumped on the sheep's backs and whispered in their ears until the sheep split into groups, reunited into a big milling pack, and went back to where they had been.

Everybody wanted a puppy. The girl sold each and every one and told them, "Go now with this new person, and be a good bitch, and remember to make your old mother proud. And if they beat you, come home to us again." And she told the people, "If ever you beat your dog, it will leave you and come home to me and you'll not get your money back, nor get your dog back either, and if you're the kind would beat a dog you're the kind would beat a woman so women, if the dog takes off, have enough sense to follow it."

Night fell before the girl got home. She had no wish to spend the night out under the stars, alone in a place where she knew nobody, so she went to the inn and paid a penny to sleep by the fire.

No sooner had she stretched out before the fire than two tawny women with golden eyes came out of the shadows carrying a big wooden chest. They laid it down near the fireplace and then they left. The young woman stared, for she had never seen tawny women with golden eyes and she knew something fey was happening. The chest opened and out came a furry grey bodach, a form of bogey, who likes to live in darkness or semi-darkness in cellars, barns, lofts, caves, attics, and old luggage which has been stored away. These bodachs are often called mischiefs.

The mischief reached out and pulled the young woman's hair and said, "You must give me tobacco to smoke and a pipe to smoke it in or I'll mischief you to the end of your days."

So she did. She had no wish to be plagued with bumps in the night or odd noises at odd times. The bodach smoked the tobacco, then grabbed the girl by the nose and said, "You must give me something decent to drink or I'll mischief you to the end of your days."

So she did. She was beginning to wish she'd slept out under the stars and taken her chances with passers-by, but she bought the bodach a drink of rum and the nasty little twerp gulped it down. The bodach hiccuped a few times, then grabbed the girl by the ear and said, "Well, now I would like a kiss and if you don't give me one, I'll mischief you to the end of your days."

So she did. And as the bodach leaned forward to kiss her, she grabbed it by the neck and choked it helpless, then tied it up with a piece of cord and stuffed it in the abersgaic.

In the morning the innkeeper asked her if she had

slept well and she said, "Oh yes, thank you very much," and off she went with her abersgaic. Soon she passed a place where the threshers were doing the grain, and when she asked them if they would do her a favour, they said they would. "It's this abersgaic," she said, "it's rubbing me raw. Could you pound on it a bit and soften it up for me, please, and if you will I'll sing you a fine song."

So they did. They put the abersgaic on the ground and started flailing it, a dozen men with a dozen flails, beating in time to the song the woman sang, and she sang a song with more verses than there are hairs on a barn cat.

When the song was finished she lifted the abersgaic and slung it on her back, then walked on down the road until she came to a place where the blacksmiths were making the tools for next year. "I'll sing you a song if you'll do me a favour," she said. "This abersgaic is rubbing my shoulders raw, could you pound on it with your big hammers for a while and soften it up."

So they did, and she sang for them while they hammered in time to the tune, and she sang them a song with more verses than there are lice on a hen.

When the song was finished she walked off down the road and the bodach inside the abersgaic begged her for mercy. "Let me go," it said, "and I will reward you with gold and silver and the finest silks."

"Oh, sure," said the young woman, "and I'll believe you and open the abersgaic and you'll leap out and curse me and mischief me to the end of my days."

"No, no," he begged, "I promise."

"You pass me some hairs from the beard on your chin," she said. For once you own the hair of a bodach, he cannot trick you, nor can any of his kin. The bodach didn't want to so the young woman said, "See, I knew you were up to something you evil old wart. Well, never mind, we're coming to another threshing crew and—" and the bodach pulled some whiskers from his beard and gave them to her. She tied them in a little knot which she pinned to her undershirt to keep her safe.

"Let me out," he said.

"No," she said, "and I will do no such thing until the rest of the promise is kept, because I know all about the tricks of such as you."

So he did. And just like that she had gold and silver, she had jewels and a fine new fiddle. And it happened they were passing by an enormous fire built in a furnace on top of which a rich man was making whiskey.

"Smell that whiskey?" the woman said.

"Ah," said the bodach, "and I'm thirsty after all that pummelling."

"Promise me," the young woman said, "that you will never mischief me or mine in this world or the next and I promise you whiskey and a good smoke."

So he did. He crossed his heart and spit three times and made incantations which could not be broken, and the girl bought a cup of the whiskey from the distillers, and poured it into the abersgaic.

"And the smoke you promised me?" the bodach bargained.

"Coming right up!" the girl said, and she pitched the abersgaic into the furnace, and the bodach and the furnace went up to the heavens as a great green flame.

# Maggy and Molly and the Clarty Little Men

O nce upon a time, not so very long ago nor so very far away, there were two countries which shared a common border. The larger of the two was ruled by a queen who had big dark eyes and long dark hair. This country had mountains and valleys, rivers and forests, and the people lived very happily, at peace with the world, or as much of the world as they knew. The other country, the smaller one, was ruled by a king who had dark eyes and a dark curly beard. The smaller country had few mountains, few valleys, few rivers, and practically no forests at all, and the many people were beginning to feel crowded.

One day the councillors, governors, generals, and members of the board of regents went to the king and told him the people were beginning to be very restless.

"Our population is too large," said one advisor.

"We have too many people and too few resources," said another.

"Every day there are more babies born, and every day there is less food to feed them," said a third.

"Well, what are we to do?" asked the king.

"Invade the next country," said the generals. "After all, they have endless miles of forest, they have valleys they don't even use yet, they have a surplus of grain and a surplus of milk and cheese, they have everything we need and they have it in rich abundance. Invade them, defeat them, and take what we need."

"There is another way," said a councillor. "Invasion always means war, and war always means killing, and it means burning and looting. It is wasteful; too many of the grain fields will burn, too many barns will be destroyed. There is another way."

And so one day the queen looked out her window and saw the king from the next country riding at the head of a very large delegation of nobles, all of them dressed in their finest clothes, each of them carrying a bouquet of flowers and a small gift-wrapped box.

The king and his men arrived at the castle, and the queen received them hospitably. She served them food and drink, she had her singers and dancers entertain them, and all seemed to be going very well.

"You have a very large country," the king said, smiling.

"Yes," the queen replied, "we have been fortunate."

"And yet your population is small," he observed.

"Small?" the queen asked. "We have never considered ourselves small."

"I have," the king said, his smile fading, "more men in my army than you have in your entire country."

"Oh," said the queen, immediately understanding everything that had been said, as well as everything that had not yet been said.

"You have a surplus of grain," the king said, "and we have a shortage of grain. You have a surplus of wheat, corn, barley, oats, milk, cheese, eggs and fish. We have shortages of everything. Except," he smiled coldly, "soldiers. We have no shortage of soldiers."

"Perhaps," the queen suggested, "if you had fewer soldiers to feed, you would have more food. Perhaps if your soldiers went out to work in the fields. . ." but the king frowned and the queen wisely bit her tongue.

"What we have in mind," the king said with a smile, "is a marriage between your country and mine. A marriage," he smiled wider, "between yourself and. . .me!"

"That isn't what I have in mind," the queen demurred.

"How much choice do you have?" the king asked, kindly enough.

"Not much," the queen admitted.

And so, with much pomp and ceremony, the marriage was announced. The king's loyal subjects were pleased; the queen's loyal subjects knew full well why their monarch had agreed to marry the king. Many of them felt she had sacrificed too much; others talked of how unnecessary it would be to have half the country laid waste in a war.

The queen had a daughter known to most people as Our Royal Princess, but called by her mother the queen simply Molly. Molly was fifteen, tall for her age, with big dark eyes and long dark hair. Molly, known also as Our Royal Princess, was not thrilled with the idea of having a stepfather, especially the one she was going to get.

The king had a daughter known to most of his subjects as Her Royal Highness, but called by her father simply Maggy. Maggy was fifteen, tall for her age, with big blue eyes and long blonde hair, for she looked like her mother, who had disappeared when Maggy was a baby.

These two royal princesses were told they were to be the maids of honour at the wedding. Maggy was quite excited about the idea of finally having a mother, and even more excited at the prospect of actually having a sister. One look at Molly's face, however, and Maggy knew her excitement was not shared.

"It's all very well and good for YOU," Molly grumbled, "after all, you get to share my mother. But what about me? I get stuck with your scowling and glowering old father!"

"He doesn't always scowl and glower," Maggy defended. "Sometimes he can be charming and witty and funny and nice."

"I," Molly glared, "have seen no sign of any of that."

"Even so," Maggy bargained, "can't you and I be friends? I've always wanted a sister."

"I am not your sister," Molly said flatly. "We can be friends, perhaps, but don't you ever forget, I am not your sister. Not REALLY."

Whatever Molly thought or didn't think about sisterhood, no sooner was the wedding ceremony over than the combined citizenry of both countries began to refer to the royal princesses as "sisters." Molly wanted to contradict everyone, she wanted to point out that she was not, after all, anybody's sister at all. But while she was more than a little bit stubborn, Molly was not stupid. She, too, knew when to bite her tongue and say nothing.

The king was very ambitious for his daughter Maggy, and wanted very much that she be given the respect and loyalty to which he felt she was entitled.

"After all," he told the queen, "there are more of my subjects that there are of yours, so it only makes sense that Maggy should have seniority over Molly."

"When you and Maggy are in your palace," the queen replied quietly, "you can have things your way. As long as you live here in my palace, things will be done my way, and I say that the girls are treated equally."

"In my palace," the king gaped. "In MY palace? That draughty old place? I am going to live here full-time, with hot and cold running water, and all the comforts. And it will be MY palace, too!"

"No," said the queen with a kind smile, "no, it is still my palace."

This stuck in the king's craw, because obviously all the courtiers, servants, housekeepers, cooks, and grooms agreed with the queen. They made it plain each and every day just whose palace this really was. The king tried to bring some of his own servants into the palace, but the truth was they were more used to living in a soldiers' barracks than they were to living in a palace, and they just did not know how to do things the way the king was getting used to having them done. The army cooks could make beans and stew, and even a roast chicken, but they could not cook the wonderful meals the queen's own cooks turned out every night. And the queen's own cooks always went to the queen to ask her what she wanted for supper; they never once asked the king. And that annoyed him terribly.

In fact, an increasing number of things annoyed the king. It annoyed him that, while his soldiers would snap to attention and salute when he passed, the people in the streets would neither cheer nor wave, but just stood, quiet and sober, watching him.

"I want a law passed," he ordered, "that everyone has to cheer when they see me."

And so a law was passed that everyone had to cheer when the king rode by on his big white horse.

And the people obeyed the law. When the king rode by, the people would obediently reach up, remove their hats, and shout "cheer."

When the queen rode by, the people jumped up and down and yelled and hollered and shouted and waved and threw flowers and sang songs and screamed HURRAY FOR THE QUEEN HURRAY HURRAY!

The king sat in his room and he fumed and he

fretted, he chewed his fingernails and he glared out the window. He saw the queen walking through the streets, mingling with the people, waving to those who waved, smiling at those who smiled, accepting flowers and kissing babies.

"You!" he shouted.

"Me?" the servant quavered.

"You! Go get Princess Molly and bring her here to me."

"Princess Molly? Don't you mean Princess Maggy, your own daughter?"

"If you want to keep your head," the king shouted, "do as you're told. Remember who it is who has the army around here."

Princess Molly went to the king's throne room and found the king sitting on his throne, wearing his crown, looking very very grim.

"Your mother and I have had a long discussion," he lied, "and it has been decided that you must start your training in earnest. You are to travel to the very end of the world. There is a lake there, and you are to bring water back from it."

"Why?" Molly asked. "We have lots and lots of good clean fresh water right here."

"Because," the king lied, "a spell was laid on your mother when you were born and if you don't go to the end of the world, find the lake, get the water, and bring it back, your mother will die."

"I'll leave right away!" Molly gasped.

And she did. She ran to her room, took off her pretty gown, and pulled on the soft brown pants she wore when she went to the stables to ride her horses or play softball with the stable workers. She pulled on a soft cotton shirt, took a warm sweater in case the weather changed, put on her good walking shoes, and tucked a spare set of socks in her pocket. Then she ran to the kitchen, grabbed a loaf of bread and a big piece of cheese to tuck in her little backpack, and set out right away for the end of the world.

Molly walked and walked and walked and walked and then she walked some more, and soon she was beyond the borders of her own country and into the country of the king. And still she walked and she walked and she walked. At night she slept wherever she could — under hedges, up in trees, in haystacks, against fences, even in caves. When she had eaten all her own food, she lived on blackberries, huckleberries, and anything else she could find.

She got very wiry and tough and suntanned, and still she walked and walked and walked, looking for the lake at the end of the world.

One day, as she was walking and picking berries, she saw a most incredible sight, an ugly little pony caught in a pricklebush, unable to go either forward or back. On its back was the most unbelievably beautiful saddle Princess Molly had ever seen in her life. A saddle of silver and gold, studded with diamonds, rubies, and emeralds, and obviously weighing a ton.

"Oh, please," said the ugly little pony, "please help me. I can go neither forward nor back, and this saddle is killing me."

"Oh, you poor wee thing," said Molly. She jumped the fence, ran across the field, and started undoing cinches and buckles and all manner of things, until the saddle fell from the pony's back and landed on the grass. "Here, now," Molly soothed, "you stand still and I'll just see what I can do about getting you out of this mess you're in."

Molly got scratched by thorns, she got scratched by prickles, she got scratched by brambles, and she even got scratched by tangles, but she got the ugly little pony out of the trap. "There," she said, looking sadly at the ripped mess that was her one and only cotton shirt. "You're free."

She stepped over the magnificent saddle, which was surely worth at least a fortune, and examined the pony. "Oh, my," she blurted, "oh, look at your poor back where that heavy thing sat for so long! Oh, that is terrible," and she began to weep. Her tears fell on the horse's back, and every place the tears fell, the poor skin of the ugly little pony healed immediately. The more Molly cried and howled, the more the little pony mended. When there were no more sores on its back, there was no more reason to cry, so Molly stopped crying, wiped her eyes, sniffled a bit, and got on with putting things right.

"Here." She took the only food she had from her pocket. "It isn't much, I know, but it's all I've been able to find so far today. We take what we can get, I suppose."

The pony ate the few berries, winked one huge blue eye at Princess Molly, and said, "Why walk to the end of the earth? Why not get up on my back and I'll carry you?"

"To the end of the earth?" Molly laughed.

"Why not?" asked the ugly little pony.

"It's a terrible far way to go," Molly smiled, "and I appreciate the offer very much, but you are a very small and very skinny pony, and while I would be proud to have you for my own, I will not ride on your back because it's sure to hurt you."

"Oh, I don't think so," the ugly little pony said. "I'm much stronger than you'd think." And—zip!—just like that, the pony changed.

Instead of a short-legged, skinny-bodied, scratched, bedraggled, ugly-looking pony, Molly was looking at a positively gargantuan dapple-grey mare with big blue eyes, a dapple-grey mare bigger, stronger, and more

119

beautiful than any horse anybody had seen since the long ago days of the faery horses. And on her back, sitting as lightly as if it had been nothing more than a pancake, the magnificent saddle made of finest leather, silver, gold, diamonds, rubies, and emeralds. And maybe even a sapphire or two.

"Now," the dapple-grey magic mare said, "do you still think I'm too small to carry you to the ends of the earth?"

"Oh, my," Molly breathed. But she was no dummy; she was up on that saddle, perched as proud as can be, smiling from ear to ear, quicker than you could tell of it. And instead of wearing old brown pants all tattered and torn, and a cotton shirt all ripped and rent, Molly was wearing nice warm dark green corduroy trousers, a nice soft cotton shirt, brand new, and a lovely little warm bright red knitted vest, which exactly matched the red knitted cap on her head.

"Hi ho," she said happily, "Hi ho and off we go!"

"There's food," the horse told her, "food in the saddlebag." And there was food, there was fried chicken and potato salad and fresh buns and orange juice, and no matter how much she ate or drank, there was always more and even more.

They moved off down the highways and byways, the roads and avenues and streets and lanes, and the miles slipped by at a great rate.

"Where do you want to spend the night?" asked the dapple-grey mare.

"Oh, anywhere will do," Molly said.

"Come, now," the horse urged. "Make a decision, don't dither. At the hotel or at the inn?"

"Neither," Molly laughed, "they both demand payment and I have no money."

"Check the saddlebags," the dapple-grey mare advised.

And you've already guessed, haven't you. All the money she would ever need. For the first time since leaving on her quest, Molly slept comfortably and warmly in a real bed in a real bedroom in the inn.

In the morning she had a very nice breakfast of pancakes, maple syrup, crispy bacon, scrambled eggs, and juice, then went out to the courtyard, swung up onto the wonderful saddle, and rode off on the back of the most beautiful horse in the world. Day after day they rode and then, suddenly, there they were, at the end of the world, where every creek, stream, and river runs into an enormous lake as big as any ocean.

Molly dismounted and stood looking down, down, down at the lake. It was surrounded, as far as her eyes could see, by steep cliffs of polished rock with neither hand-hold nor foot-hold. Somehow she had to get down those cliffs with a container, get the water, climb back up the cliffs, and take the water home to save her mother's life. But how?

"How will I ever get down?" she asked the beautiful dapple-grey mare, but the mare just looked at her as if she had never in her life been able to speak, and Molly realized that this time she was on her own.

She sat down on the grass to ponder her predicament and, after a very few minutes, realized she could hear moaning and whimpering and sniffling. She got up and looked around and there, in a fissure in the cliff, were three little men, no bigger than dwarfs, all clarty and dirty and tangle-haired and weeping.

"What's wrong?" she called to them.

"We cannot get down and we cannot get up," one of them wept.

"We cannot go to the left nor yet go to the right,"another one mourned.

"We're stuck," the third said bitterly.

"Just a minute," Molly blurted. She got her warm

sweater and began to unravel it, first the collar, then the sleeves, then the body, and finally the ribbed waistband, and when there was no more sweater, but only a big ball of wool, she began to lower the wool over the side of the cliff.

"Gently, gently," she called, "don't break the wool."

The smallest of the clarty little men took hold of the slender piece of wool and—zip!—instead of a piece of wool he had a strong piece of rope in his hand. When the second took hold, the strong piece of rope became an even stronger ladder, and when the third grabbed on, the ladder grew and grew and grew until it reached right down to the banks of the huge lake at the very end of the world.

The three little filthy men clambered down the ladder to the side of the lake, and Molly followed them.

"What luck!" she laughed. "But who are you?"

"We are the guardians of the end of the world," said the first.

"It is our duty to ensure that only the pure of heart have access to the lake," said the second.

"Those who refuse to help us get no help from us," the third said firmly.

"Will you wash me?" asked the first filthy little man.

"Will you scrub me clean?" asked the second clarty little gnome.

"Will you dry me with your own hair?" asked the third.

"Well," said Molly, pointing at the lake, "there's a world of water there, why don't you wash yourselves?"

"Well," the first confessed, "we can't. There's a spell on us, you see."

"We'll stay ugly little dirty men until a beautiful virgin will do as we've asked," said the second.

"As you can see," the third mourned, "in over a thousand years, nobody has!"

Molly thought about what it would be like to be small, deformed, ugly, and filthy dirty for a thousand years.

"Come on," she said. She picked up the first filthy little man and put him in the water. She washed him from head to toe, scrubbing behind his ears, between his toes, and around his neck until he was clean all over, even his hair. "You're next," she said, and she took hold of the second filthy little gnome and did the same with him. "Now you," she smiled, and it was the third clarty little man's turn. And when all three of them were as clean as clean can be, they joined hands and danced in a circle and sang.

Iddle diddle diddle di diddle dee dum
Da rum pa diddle diddle da rum dum dum

"I'll make you ten times prettier than you are," the first one offered.

"Oh, no," said Molly, "you don't have to give me a present. It was just a friendship favour I did you, and your friendship is as much payment as I want."

"Wouldn't you like to be ten times prettier?" he coaxed.

"Actually," she laughed, "I'm quite satisfied with how I look now."

"I'll fix it so every time you open your mouth, diamonds and rubies pour out," the second one offered.

"Oh, no, thank you," Molly said, "then I'd never be able to sing. It was a friendship favour I did you, and your friendship is worth more to me than all the diamonds and rubies in the world."

"I could arrange it that every time you brushed your hair, gold and silver would fall from it," the third offered.

"Oh, no, thank you," Molly said for the third time, "it was a friendship favour I did you, and your friendship is all the treasure I could want."

The three little men looked at her, then looked at each other and nodded. "And would you comb my hair for me," asked the first, with absolutely no trace of a smile at all.

"Of course," said Molly, "except I have no comb and will have to use my fingers."

So she used her fingers as a comb, and in an amazingly short period of time, the first little man's wild and bushy hair was neat and tidy and hanging in two braids below his shoulders.

"And my beard?" asked the second, with absolutely no trace of smile at all.

Molly was getting a bit impatient but, after all, she had fussed the first, so she could hardly say no to the second. She used her fingers to comb out the messy tangle of gingery beard, and when it was combed out and tidy, she put a knot in the bottom of it to keep the wind from blowing it around and tangling it again.

"And what," the third asked, with absolutely no trace of a smile, "what about my toenails?"

"I don't have any scissors," Molly said. And quick as a flash, the little gnome did something magic and handed Molly a sharp sword.

"You can," he said softly, "cut my toe nails with this. Or you could lop off my head."

"Lop off your head?" she asked. "And why would I want to do that?"

"Then you wouldn't have to cut my toenails," he said flatly.

"I don't HAVE to cut them now," Molly said firmly. "The only things I HAVE to do in my life are get the water from the lake and take it back so my mother won't die, and, when it is time, die myself."

So she took the sharp sword and cut the toenails of the third, and though his toenails were the only ones she cut, the toenails of the other two were suddenly short and clean.

"There," she said, and she smiled, no longer impatient with the three demanding little men. "There, you look quite lovely."

And just like that—zip!—before anything else could be said or done, the three little men started to talk to each other. "Blether, dether, dribble, flibble," they said, only it wasn't blether at all, nor dether either, and it certainly wasn't dribble or flibble, it just sounded that way because it was a language Molly could not understand. "Rimble rumble bimble bumble," they said, and—poof!—three of the sidhe stood there, three of the magic women who at one time inhabited the entire world. And one had blonde hair, one had black hair, and one had hair the colour of arbutus bark.

"Why you aren't ugly little men at all!" Molly blurted.

"Not at all," agreed the sidhe.

"Then why did you pretend to..."

"We are the guardians of the end of the earth," they said, "but we are more than that. We are the guardians of truth and of unselfishness, and our reasons are not always easily understood. But you have been kind and, more importantly, you have been patient. You did what we asked, and did more. You even smiled as you did it."

And gurgle gurgle, the water from the lake at the end of the world came bubbling up and formed itself into a crystal clear urn, then filled the urn, and as Molly reached out to take it, the urn carried her up, up, up the cliff and set her on the beautiful saddle on the back of the wonderful dapple-grey mare.

It had taken a long long time to get from the palace to the lake at the end of the world, but the trip back took no time at all. In less than a blink of an eye they were back at the place where she had seen the ugly little pony trapped in the bramble berries. "Whoa," said Molly, "I'll get off now, thank you very very much, and you can be free."

"Why not just keep me?" asked the dapple-grey mare.

"Well, it wouldn't be right, would it?" Molly said, a tear glinting in her eye. "After all, you offered to take me to the end of the world, and you did that. And now we're back, and you've more than repaid me for the little favour I did you."

No sooner were the words out of her mouth than the three sidhe women were there, smiling at her and nodding approval.

"This is not the first decent thing you've done," they said. "You saved an ugly pony, that's one decent thing. You wept to see the sores on its back, that's two decent things. You healed it, and that's a third decent thing. You helped us out of the fissure, that's four decent things. You washed us, that's five, six, and seven decent things. You combed hair is eight decent things; you combed beard, that's nine decent things; you cut toenails is ten decent things. And now you offer to free the horse is eleven decent things. One day, Molly, you will be rewarded for the decent things you have done." And — pop! — they were gone again.

"If you don't mind," the great dapple-grey mare said, "I would like to accompany you. I have never been in a royal procession. It might be fun."

"Any time you want to be free," Molly promised, "just go."

They rode up to the palace and Molly turned the great dapple-grey mare loose in the royal stables, and told the stable boys to give the mare the best of everything. Then, still dressed in corduroy pants, cotton shirt, red vest, and red cap, she went into the palace, to the king's throne room.

"What are you doing back here?" he shouted. "I thought I told you to—"

"You did," Molly said easily. "And I did. And I got it. And here it is," and she handed him the jug of water.

"What's that?" asked the queen.

"It's water from the lake at the very end of the world," Molly said happily, "and now the spell that was put on you is broken and you won't die."

"Die?" said the queen. "Who? Me? Die? Well, one day I will, we all do, but not because of any spell. And even if there had been a spell, I would rather have died than have sent you to the very end of the earth, through dangers and trials and who-knows-what."

And the jug wrenched itself from the king's hands and flew through the air, and when it was directly over the lap of the queen, it tipped itself and the water poured from within. But before the water drenched the queen's gown, it was transformed into a stream of gold.

"Now," said Molly, who had grown a great deal wiser on her trip, "now we can show the gold to the king's soldiers and offer to pay them if only they will fight for US instead of for HIM."

The king knew his days in the palace were not going to be many, and he jumped from his throne, ran from the throne room, called for his horse, jumped on it, and raced off, ordering as many of his men to follow him as he could.

The army, of course, did not know what had transpired in the throne room, and they had not yet been offered a reward to disobey the king, so all the soldiers and generals jumped on their horses and followed. Maggy, being a dutiful and obedient daughter, got on her horse and went along with the rest.

Back in his own palace, the king began to scheme and to plan. He heard of the wonderful dapple-grey

127

mare Princess Molly had, and he heard of the beautiful saddle, and he put two and two together, and decided she had found them at the end of the world where she had got the water.

So he called Princess Maggy to his throne room. "I am sending you to the very end of the earth," he commanded. "And I want you to bring back a jug of water from the lake that lies there."

"Father—" Maggy had a question to ask, but she never got to ask it.

"Go!" he said. "You have half an hour to get ready."

Maggy was very puzzled, but she went to her room and got herself ready to go to the end of the world. She put on warm trousers, a sturdy shirt, good walking boots, and a jacket, then filled a backpack with bread and cheese and a pitcher of juice, and she headed off down the road, looking for the end of the world and the lake that lay there.

Not far from the palace, no more than a four or five day walk, Maggy saw an ugly little pony with a huge saddle on its bleeding back, and the pony was caught in the briars and brambles.

"Oh, my," said Maggy.

"Please," sobbed the pony, "please help me."

Maggy ran over, dropped her pack and her jacket, and undid the cinch to dump the beautiful saddle to the ground. Next she started snapping the vines and the brambles and the tendrils and the briars that held the little ugly pony prisoner. She got her hands cut, she got her fingers scratched, she got her wrists and arms ripped, and she bled, but she got the little pony out of the tangle.

The little pony stepped out of the briars and nodded its head thank you, but Maggy saw the sores on its back, and the blood running from them, and just as Molly had done, Maggy began to weep. "Oh, you poor

poor little thing," she said, "oh, just look what that dreadful heavy saddle has done to you." And where her tears fell, the sores healed, just as it had been when Molly wept. And the more Maggy wept and cried and sobbed and howled, the more the sores on the pony's back healed, and when there were no more sores there was no more reason to cry, so Maggy quit crying just as Molly had done.

"Here," she said, bringing out the last of her food. "Here, I know it isn't much, but I'm sure you can use it, you look quite hungry."

The ugly little pony ate the crust of bread, then winked one eye at Maggy and said, "Get up on my back and I'll give you a ride."

"No, thank you." Maggy patted the shaggy head. "I have a long long way to go, all the way to the ends of the earth, and that is much too much for a little pony like you."

"Oh, I don't think so," the pony laughed and—zip!— just like that, the pony changed. Instead of a short-legged, skinny-bodied, scratched, bedraggled, and ugly-looking pony, Maggy was looking at a positively enormous buckskin mare with lovely blue eyes, a buckskin mare bigger, stronger, and more beautiful than any Maggy had ever seen. And on the buckskin's back there was a beautiful saddle of fine leather, gold, silver, diamonds, rubies, and emeralds. And maybe even a sapphire or two.

"Now," the buckskin mare said, "do you still think I'm too small to carry you to the very ends of the earth?"

"Oh, my," Maggy breathed, "oh, you are beyond doubt capable of anything at all."

She swung herself up on the buckskin's back and the horse set off down the road. Now magic horses are capable of anything at all, even travelling through time as well as through space. And in the wink of an eye, or so it seemed, there they were, Maggy and the buckskin, atop the cliff, looking down at the lake which lay at the very end of the earth.

Maggy dismounted and looked down, down, down at the lake. It was surrounded as far as her eyes could see by steep polished cliffs which offered neither hand-hold nor toe-hold.

"How in the world will I ever get down?" she wondered, but the buckskin mare had nothing at all to say to her.

Maggy sat down on the grass to ponder her predicament and, after a very few moments, realized she could hear moaning and groaning and mewling and whimpering and sniffling and snoffling and sounds of great lamentation. She looked around and there, in a fissure in the rocks, were three very dirty little men, no bigger than dwarfs, all clarty and tangle-haired and weeping and unsightly.

"What's wrong?" she called to them.

"We cannot get down and we cannot get up," one of them wept.

"We cannot go to the left nor yet go to the right," the second one mourned.

"We're stuck," the third said bitterly.

"Just a minute," Maggy blurted. She got her jacket and began to tear it into strips, and when she had nothing left but a pile of strips, she knotted the strips into one long strip and lowered it over the edge of the cliff.

"Gently, gently," she called. "I don't know how strong this is."

The smallest of the clarty little men took hold of the strip and—zip!—instead of a knotted strip he had a strong piece of rope. When the second clarty little man took hold, the strong piece of rope became an even stronger ladder, and when the third grabbed on, the ladder grew and grew and grew until it reached right down to the banks of the huge lake at the very end of the world.

The three filthy little men clambered down the ladder to the side of the lake, and Maggy, who was no fool, clambered down with them.

"What luck," she said. "What wonderful luck! Who are you?"

"Well, we're the guardians of the end of the world," said the first.

"It is our duty to ensure that only those who are pure of heart have access to the lake," said the second.

"Those who refuse to help us get no help from us," the third said firmly.

"Will you wash me?" asked the first filthy little man.

"Will you scrub me clean?" asked the second clarty little gnome.

"Will you dry me with your own hair?" asked the third.

"Well," said Maggy, "one would think that with your being the guardians of the lake, you would have all the water in the world to clean yourselves."

"We can't," the first sighed. "There's a spell on us, you see."

"We'll stay ugly and dirty until a beautiful virgin comes along and does as we ask," the second replied.

"As you can see," the third mourned, "we are a terrible mess."

"You are indeed," Maggy agreed. "You look as if it's been a thousand years or more since you were clean and tidy."

"Not quite," the first said with a small smile.

Maggy picked up the first dirty little dwarf, plunked him in the lake, and scrubbed him from head to toe, even checking inside his ears and paying particular attention to his elbows and knees. When he was clean, she dried him with her hair and sat him on a sun-warmed rock. Then she picked up the second filthy little troll and did the same to him, and when he was done, it was the turn of the third.

No sooner were they clean than they joined hands and danced in a circle, singing.

Iddle diddle diddle di diddle dee dum
Da rum pa diddle diddle da rum dum dum

"I'll make you ten times prettier than you are," the first offered.

"No, thank you," Maggy laughed. "I might not be much, but I'm me and that's good enough. Anyway, you don't owe me anything. It was a friendship favour and your friendship is all the payment anyone could want."

"I'll fix it so every time you open your mouth, diamonds and rubies tumble out," the second one promised.

"No, thank you," Maggy smiled, "then I wouldn't be able to laugh without choking, and I wouldn't be able to talk to my friends. What I did was done for friendship, and I want no reward."

"I could arrange it that every time you brushed your hair, gold and silver would fall from it," the third offered.

"Oh, no, thank you, it was friendship and friendship only prompted me to give you a bath, and I truly do not need any reward."

"Then will you comb my hair for me?" the first asked, with absolutely no trace of a smile on his face.

"Comb your hair? Well, if that'll put a smile on your face, of course I will." And she used her fingers to comb his hair, and when it was neat and tidy, she pulled it back and plaited one long braid down his back. "There," she said, "you look quite handsome."

"What about my tangled-up beard?" the second one demanded, rather rudely.

"Your beard? You can't look after your own beard? Well, come here, then." Maggy picked him up, sat him on a sun-warmed rock, and began to tidy his beard. "You really should learn how to do this yourself," she said gently, "you can't stay a baby all your life."

"And what about my toenails?" the third mourned.

"My dear wee friend," Maggy said carefully, "I don't know about your toenails. I have no scissors to cut them."

And as if by magic (which, indeed, it was), the little gnome handed Maggy a wickedly sharp sword.

"You can," he said softly, "cut my toenails with this. Or you could lop off our heads and claim the lake for your own."

"Whyever would I want to claim your lake for my own?" Maggy asked.

"Well, the king claimed the land of the queen as his own," the gnarly little dwarf replied.

"I don't know anything at all about any of that," Maggy said. "I only know I was sent here for water." Very carefully she cut the long filthy toenails of the third little man. No sooner had she cut his toenails than the toenails of the others were short and clean.

"There," Maggy said, "now you all look quite respectable and presentable."

And like that—zip!—the three little men began to talk to each other. "Blether blether dether dribble fibble fubble dee," only it was none of that at all, it just sounded like that because Maggy couldn't understand their language. "Rimble rumble bimble bumble," they said, and—poof!—three sidhe stood there, the magic women who at one time inhabited the entire world. And one had blonde hair, one had black hair, and one had hair the colour of arbutus bark.

"Something more is happening than I first thought!" Maggy blurted.

And the three magic women told her what they had told Molly, and gurgle gurgle, the water from the lake came up and poured into Maggy's pitcher, then the pitcher lifted her up, up, up to the top of the cliff and set her down gently on the gorgeous saddle on the back of the beautiful buckskin mare.

In less time than it takes to tell, they were back at the place where Maggy had freed the ugly little pony trapped in the tangleberries.

"Whoa," said Maggy, "I'll get off now, thank you very much."

"Why not keep me?" asked the buckskin mare.

"Keep you? How can I keep you?" Maggy asked. "You were free when I first saw you and it would be wrong not to leave you as free as when I found you."

No more were the words out of her mouth than the sidhe women were there, nodding approval and smiling.

"This is not the first decent thing you've done," they said. "You saved an ugly pony, you wept to see the sores on its back, you healed it, you helped us out of the fissure, you washed us, you combed hair, you combed beard, you cut toe nails, and now you offer to free the horse. That is eleven decent things you have done. One day you will be rewarded for all the decent things you did." And—pop!—they were gone again.

"Come," said the buckskin mare, "let us ride to the palace."

"Any time you want to be free," Maggy said, "just go."

They rode toward the palace. At first, Maggy did not notice that anything was any different, but gradually she realized that nobody seemed to see her. She was used to being seen. She was, after all, the Princess of the Realm, and her father had given orders that the people were to cheer and wave. But today, Maggy rode down the road and nobody took any notice.

"What is happening?" she asked the buckskin horse.

"We can move through time and space," the horse replied easily, "and we can move invisibly. And today I think you should take advantage of the invisibility to see for yourself how things Really are."

"What do you mean?"

"Do you remember when the sidhe asked you if you would like to kill them and claim the lake for your own? And you said no, you wouldn't do that? And they asked why not, for your father had taken the land of the queen? And you said. . ."

"I said I knew nothing of any of that."

"It is time to find out some of that," the buckskin mare said firmly.

Maggy sat on the buckskin mare and used her eyes. She saw soldiers sitting together drinking beer, she saw soldiers sitting together eating food, she saw soldiers sitting together playing dice games, and she saw ordinary people working, working, working, working to try to wrench from the soil enough food to feed all the soldiers. She saw entire mountainsides where all the trees had been cut down and the land left bare. She saw rivers that had been sullied and dirtied by having the army race back and forth from one side to the other.

"I think I am beginning to understand some things," Maggy said quietly.

The buckskin mare took Maggy to the palace of the king, and Maggy went inside carrying the pitcher of lake water.

"Give that here," said the king, and he took it and poured it on the floor. The water came from the pitcher and before it landed on the royal carpet, the water turned to gold.

135

"Wonderful!" said the king. But when he reached to grab the gold, he cried out in pain and jerked back his hand, his fingers blistered and burned.

"Not for you," said a voice. He whirled and the sidhe stood there in mid-air, laughing at him. "Not for you. Either get your own or get it for someone you love. Molly got hers because she loves her mother and didn't want her to die. And Maggy got hers because she's afraid of you. You either get it for yourself or get it for someone you love, and since she's afraid of you and doesn't love you, she got it for her, and if you want some, go get your own."

The king shouted and yelled insults, but the sidhe don't care a fig for any of that, and in the end the king called for his army and his councillors and his retinue and all the things he thought important, and he set off to find the lake at the end of the earth. Just to make sure he got enough of the lake water to give him all the gold he wanted, he took every washtub, bathtub, bucket, pail, pitcher, kettle, and cup in the kingdom with him.

The three sidhe turned to Maggy and asked her if she had any questions.

"Yes," Maggy said. "I have more questions than there are answers. Why is it I don't love my father? And how is it that I have no mother? And why did my mother love a man who is so . . . unpleasant?"

The sidhe looked at each other and talked to each other in their own language for a while, and then—poof!—in the air outside the window, Maggy saw pictures. She saw a beautiful young woman holding hands with a handsome young man, as they walked in an orchard of apple trees. She saw an arrow fly through the air and pierce the breast of the handsome young man, and she saw him fall to the grass and die. Then she saw the man she thought was

her father step out from behind an apple tree,
laughing, and holding in his hand a bow, the very bow
which had shot the arrow that killed the handsome
young man.

"Who is the young woman?" she asked.

"Your mother," said the first sidhe.

"And the handsome young man?"

"Your father," replied the second sidhe.

"And the man I thought was my father is not?" Maggy
asked.

"You saw what happened," the third sidhe said.

"And where is my mother now?" Maggy asked, and
her voice was suddenly very strong and very firm.

"She is kept prisoner in a tower beyond the far hills,"
the sidhe said.

Quick as a flash, Maggy ran from the palace and
leapt on the back of the beautiful buckskin mare. "Take
me to the tower beyond the far hills and I will give you
every ounce of gold I possess!" she promised.

"What would I want with gold?" the buckskin mare
asked. "I'll take you anywhere you want to go, my
friend, but do not bother me with gold," and they were
off, racing faster than the wind.

It happened that just then Molly was out riding her
beautiful dapple-grey mare, galloping through the
forest, enjoying every minute of the beautiful day.
Then she heard the sound of rapidly galloping hooves.

"And what is chasing you?" she called.

"Nothing," Maggy answered. "I'd explain but I'm in a
hurry!"

"I'll ride with you," Molly offered, her curiosity
aroused.

"You won't be able to keep up," Maggy warned.

But of course Molly and her dapple-grey mare had
no trouble at all keeping up with Maggy and her
buckskin mare, and while they raced toward the tower

hidden in the far hills, Maggy explained to Molly all that the sidhe had shown and revealed to her.

"Now," she said, "I must free my mother."

"And I will help!" Molly said firmly. "I know how I would feel if it was my mother locked in a tower hidden in the far hills."

The two magnificent horses got them to the tower in no time flat, and the two princesses looked up, up, up, up to the very top of the tower. And up there, so high it was almost hidden in the clouds, was a little room, and from that room they could hear the sound of a woman singing a sad and lonely song.

"Mother!" Maggy called. "Mother, it's Maggy!" A face appeared at the window of the little room at the top of the tower.

"Maggy?" a voice asked. "Maggy? Really?"

"Yes, really," Maggy answered. "I'll get you out of that room."

"No," said her mother. "No, you must not try! Nobody has ever been able to climb this high. It is too dangerous! You will get hurt! Better I stay a prisoner forever than you risk your life."

"How can I live a full and happy life knowing my mother is a prisoner?" Maggy demanded.

"And yet," her mother said, "from up here in this tower I can see my people, and they are toiling in the fields and in the factories, prisoners of their own condition in life, and not matter how hard they work, they never get ahead because the army takes everything. And all those people who are trapped in misery are the mothers and fathers of somebody or other!"

"Madame Queen," Molly said carefully, but loudly enough to be heard up at the top of the tower. "Madame Queen, if you please, one thing at a time. You first; the others later." And she got off her dapple-grey mare and moved to climb up the tower.

"Stop!" a voice ordered, and then—zip!—the sidhe were there, one with blonde hair, one with black hair, and one with hair the colour of arbutus bark. "Why are you going to risk your life to someone else's mother?" they asked.

"How can I feel free if I know someone else is locked in a tower?" Molly asked reasonably. "Surely you three can't just stand by and let this kind of thing go unquestioned."

"That is twelve," said the first sidhe.

"A full twelve," the second agreed.

"At least twelve," the third smiled, "and decent things deserve to be rewarded."

They joined hands and began chanting in their own language, and with every strange syllable, the tower shrank smaller and smaller and smaller until it was no height at all, and the imprisoned queen was standing before them, staring at her daughter and smiling through her tears.

The queen rode behind Maggy on the beautiful buckskin mare, all the way back to the palace. The people looked up from their work and forgot how tired they were, all the aches and pains seemed to disappear, they smiled, they took off their hats and caps and threw them in the air and cheered. "The queen! The queen!" and some even cheered, "Hurrah for the queen and the princess!"

Meanwhile, of course, the king was thundering off with his army, heading for the end of the world, to the lake into which flows all the water of the earth, the water that is more precious than gold.

Suddenly the king saw a little donkey standing trapped in the brambles, and on its back was a ten-ton saddle made of silver, gold, diamonds, and all manner of precious jewels.

"Help," the little donkey begged. "Oh, please, sir, help me."

"Shut up!" said the king. He got off his horse, took off his own saddle, threw it in the ditch, and took the heavy saddle from the donkey. Then he got fifteen soldiers to help him lift the ten-ton saddle of gold and silver up onto the back of his own poor horse.

"Help," said the donkey.

"I said shut up!" the king shouted. "I will not be spoken to by a donkey!" And he swung himself up on the ten-ton saddle, intending to ride on to the end of the earth.

But it was too much for the poor horse, which fell over sideways because of the ten-ton saddle and the weight of the king.

The soldiers wanted to laugh, but did not dare. Even if he was dumped on his backside in the dust, he was still their king. So they helped him up, dusted him off, found another horse for him, and rode off, leaving the poor little donkey still trapped in the tangles.

When they were well and truly out of sight, the little donkey stepped out of the bramble bush and—zip!—changed into the most absolutely beautiful big black mare anybody could imagine. Tossing her head contemptuously, she walked away from the bramble patch and headed down the road toward the palace of the queen.

Eventually the king and his army arrived at the very end of the earth, where all the water from all the creeks, rivers, streams, lakes, ponds, and ditches goes. And, of course, the king had to dismount and study the problem of getting down the cliff to the lake shore.

He heard the sound of weeping and wailing, looked over the edge, and saw the three filthy little men in the crack in the cliff.

"Shut up," said the king. "Your noise bothers me."

"Help us, please," said the first.

"Help us, sir," said the second.

"We're trapped," said the third.

"Don't bother me," said the king. "I have important business here!"

"But we cannot go left or right," said the first.

"We can go neither up nor down," said the second.

"We can go neither in nor out," said the third.

"Stop your bleating and wailing," the king raged. "How can a person think with all that yammering going on?" And he picked up a big rock and dropped it over the edge of the cliff. The rock fell almost on top of the three little men, and just when it looked as if they would be crushed to death, the rock flew back up, exactly in the direction it had just come. And it caught the king under the chin, knocked him backside over appetite in the dirt. His crown fell off and rolled over the edge of the cliff into the lake.

"Get that crown!" the king screeched.

His army ran to the edge of the cliff to try to grab the crown, and the rock that had knocked the king on his bum came swirling around again and smashed into them, knocking them one on top of the other in a big tangle of arms and legs and noses and ears and even a tongue and an eyebrow or two.

"You fools!" The king jumped up, ran over to the tangle that was his army, and began to kick at the soldiers, trying to kick them apart.

And the water in the lake at the very end of the earth began to roil and boil, to foam and thunder, to toss and tumble, and then it formed itself into a great big fist, an absolutely humungous fist of water at the end of a thick arm of seething waves, and — gurgle! — they were all gone except the horses. Gone the soldiers, gone the generals, gone the king himself.

At the very instant the evil king and his army were snatched up by the great water fist, the sidhe appeared at the palace of the first queen, she who was the

141

mother of Princess Molly. And two eye blinks later, Princess Maggy and her mother appeared, looking very surprised and even a bit frightened.

"So," said the sidhe with blonde hair, "here we have two princesses and two queens and two countries."

"And," said the sidhe with the black hair, "the Princesses have some favours coming to them."

"What do you want for your first favour?" the sidhe with hair the colour of arbutus bark asked Princess Molly.

"All I want is that my mother live a long and happy life, and when it is time for her to die, I want her to die peacefully and with no pain."

"And for yourself?" the sidhe asked.

"I'm fine," Molly laughed. "I have a song to sing and a beautiful friend of a horse to ride, and I even have found myself a friend who is as close and as dear to me as a sister." She reached over to take Princess Maggy's hand in hers. "I'm sorry," she said, suddenly shy. "I'm sorry I ever said you weren't my real sister."

"Thirteen," said the sidhe in surprise and wonder. "Thirteen decent things from one young woman!"

"And you?" they asked Princess Maggy. "What favour would you like to have first?"

"I want my mother to live a full and happy life, and to forget the years of sorrow when she was trapped in that tower."

"And for yourself?"

"Oh, I have everything I need," Maggy said. "I have the most beautiful horse in the entire world, and I have a mother I thought I had lost, and I have a sort-of stepmother, even if she wasn't really married to my really father because...it does get very mixed-up, doesn't it?" she laughed. "And I have Molly for my friend and sister. I don't think I need anything else."

"If the princesses will not take their favours," the

sidhe with hair the colour of arbutus bark said, "perhaps the queens would consider taking some?"

"I don't think we really need any magic favours," Maggy's mother said. "I think if we work together in friendship, we can sort out most of this mess by ourselves."

"The army is gone," Molly's mother said happily, "and until the damage they caused is repaired, well, we do have a surplus, and we can certainly share with our neighbours."

"I propose we agree there will be no army," said one queen.

"No army at all," said the other queen.

"And we'll clean up the rivers and replant the forests and. . ." They began to make plans.

"And what about you?" the sidhe asked the two young women.

"I want to travel the land, listening to the people and finding out what it is they really want out of life," said one princess, and it doesn't matter whether it was Maggy or whether it was Molly.

So the two young women put clean clothes and plenty of food into their packs, then kissed their mothers goodbye, then each kissed the mother of the other goodbye, and they went outside and climbed up to sit on the beautiful saddles on the backs of the wonderful horses. And they set off together, singing happily, on the first of a new series of adventures.

The sidhe sat down with the two queens to have tea and cakes and to help in the planning of a peaceful future for the two lands.

And nobody missed the evil king or his army.

# After the Mad King Died

In that time after the mad king died
and before my mother and sisters were taken
the wyccan took me and instead of dyeing
my entire body blue, as was custom, they
introduced me to Morgana, the shapeshifter,
the changeable, the transformed, the transformer
and then a dark blue mark was put on my body,
put on in such a way it looked natural, and might
have been anything, a freckle, a mole, a birthmark,
a bruise, but I knew, and they knew, and Ceridwen
knew and I would be recognized even after death
by that mark, that special mark.
And when eighty thousand Celtic souls
went to join the crone mother
it was I, the third daughter, the youngest,
the one never intended to rule
who took my mother and my sisters
and left that cursed place.
Do you know a family named Hicks
or a family named Hickock
or a family named Hickle
or any family of any such name?

144

Then you know people
descended of those who died.
And while the Hiccan villages burned
and Hiccan blood was spilled
I sat in the corricle, my hair unbound,
my heart breaking, and the wind and tide
took us all, my mother, my sisters, and I
to that place of death
that island whose very name
means honour and courage
bravery and truth
and the women there came to the pebble beach
and received the last remains
of the queen who honoured the queen of all Britain.
They opened the burrows and went into the
    underground
taking my flame-haired mother and golden sisters
and I had to wait outside
until it was done.
And when it was done, it was done properly,
and it was all done, and the burrow closed,
and I was alone with the women
who live their lives in the service of the Crone.

They taught me to hide
they taught me to be clever
they taught me the secrets
of rings and of circles
of spirals and of colours
and when I knew
practically nothing of what they knew
they told me
I could go, that the secrets were safe

and I was alone

They negotiated with Prasatagus and thought him the
    king,
he who was no king at all but a pet, a toy, a mockery
put in place for no reason other than to be deposed
by whichever of the strong young men my eldest sister
    chose,
and Prasatagus, flattered, agreed that half of
    everything
would be given to Nero. In return, Nero's legions
protected Prasatagus, known as pimpleface, known as
    pathetic.
Prasatagus died. Suddenly. Predictably. And Rome
    sent the eagles
to raid and steal, to murder and confiscate, to kidnap
    and
transport Celtic youth to the arenas where they were
doomed to a short life as gladiators and gladiatrix,
they who had been chosen of the oak and of the
    hawthorne.
And Boadicea protested, outraged, she who was queen
    and
owed allegiance to the queen of all Britain, she of the
copper-streaked hair and sea-changing eyes, she of the
great height and powerful limb, she whose voice
was like the voice of the black ravens of Ceridwen,
calling roughly and unafraid, slivering the day
into fragments, measuring the turning of the years.
Go away, she said, and leave these shores, a peaceful
    people
when angered make deadly enemies, go away and leave
us
to our fields and our barley, to our houses and our
    children
for you are no longer welcome under this mist blue
    sky.
The eagle took her, tied her where all could see
and scourged her with whips, flogging her until

blood poured from her back and the flesh
was laid open to the bone. She bit on her forearm
to deny them the pleasure of hearing her scream,
bit until blood flowed and her throat swelled,
veins extended, and those of us mustered to watch
this abomination began to sing, our voices rising loud
that no Roman bastard would hear our queen moan
    with pain.
—hey derry down derry derry derry down hey derry
    down derry down—
My two sisters were dragged out and thrown to the
    ground
at our mother's bleeding feet, then, before our
    disbelieving eyes
they were repeatedly raped by the gentleman soldiers
    of Rome
to prove, they said, there is no power in women
no power greater than that of man who can impose his
    will
on and even in any woman who walks.
The holy people heard of this and rose up and Paulinus
    Suetonius
went after them, with his horses and chariots, his
    fierce dogs
of war, and his brown robed chanting idiot priests
and my mother made her move. First Colchester, then
    London itself,
and all those who had known the truth but rejected it
to curry favour with the invaders were taken to the
    sacred grove
and sent off to that other place where Ceridwen will
    judge them
and her black dogs with the red eyes and white fangs
will measure the truth and pay the debts.
Suetonius headed back to London, followed by the last
    few Druids,

147

and when he saw my mother's army, he abandoned
     Londonius completely
and the place was levelled in rubble.
An entire Roman legion was slaughtered, six thousand
     Romans
including cavalry and my mother symbolically
pissed on them, their flags and banners trampled.
But we paid dearly, and the earth was turned to mud
because of the lifeblood we spilled.
We were not warriors, not professional mercenaries,
we were farmers, tillers of fields, herders and weavers,
singers of songs and memorizers of ballads,
but we moved against the eagle, vicious carrion eater,
offal feaster, bird who lives on decaying flesh.
Suetonius told his legions all Celts are women,
and regaled them with stories of women loving
     women,
and my mother told her people she did not command
     them as a queen
nor say they must risk their lives for her wealth, with
     them
or without them, she, a woman, would fight for her
     freedom,
fight to avenge the scars corded and thick on her back,
fight to avenge her daughters, fight to protect their
     daughters,
fight to protect the aged and the weak, to save our
     youth
from the arenas and our lands from the metal plow.
One legion had perished, another would follow, she
     said,
you do not collect this many loyal and loving allies
through threats and fear. Victory, she said, or death,
but never life as a slave, and we closed with them,
women, children, men, we closed with the legions,
and eighty thousand Celts died that day, died and

were taken by the transforming ravens, taken
back to the cauldron and passed through it,
taken to Ceridwen by Morgana. A few of us were
    passed over,
denied passage to Avalon, denied the apple of
    immortality,
and the eagle came after us, demanding to know
where my mother was buried. Village after village was
searched, burned, the people killed, and still the
    Romans
could not find her grave, could not defile her earthly
    remains,
nor did they ever find the bodies of my sisters, whom
    my
mother herself killed, to spare them further
    defilement.

and the enemy
searches us yet

# AVALON

---

Long ago and far away there was a magical land where the human people and the little people lived together harmoniously. The clean life-giving ocean waves lapped sandy beaches where children played and the fisherwomen and fishermen set out every day in their small boats to cast their nets and drop their lines. Magnificent forests marched from the high tide line across the surface of the earth, over hills and ridges, and up the steep sides of massive mountains.

The people lived in the valleys along the banks of clean rivers, and planted their crops in deep, rich soil. Fruit trees blossomed in the spring, and every autumn the people harvested a bounty of apples, pears, plums, and other delicious fruit. Birds of every sort lived in the trees, flew through the air, and filled the days with song, while butterflies and ladybugs were so tame they would happily land on the hand of a small child.

The brownies and boggarts and gnomes and gremlins and kobolds and goolyguys worked in their own ways to help the human people, and the pixies, piscies, nixies and elves danced, sang and entertained everybody.

But then things began to change, and not for the better. The gremlins had taught human people how to make tools, and had whispered gremlin secrets into the ears of inventors so it became possible to make machines which could do many of the jobs human people had once done. The humans gave no credit to the gremlins, and paid no attention to the gremlin rules, and so the machines began to proliferate, and some of the human people forgot how to behave properly.

The human people began to cut down the magnificent forests, and the poor nymphs and wood sprites were left homeless. The dryads had no place to sleep, the nyads were lost and confused, and the leshies were working overtime trying to confuse the woodcutters and get them so lost they gave up and went back home again, sparing the forest.

But the woodcutters continued to cut down trees and without the great roots to hold the soil in place, the rain washed it into the streams and rivers, making the water muddy, ruining the home of the nixies and sprites, and disturbing the kelpies and the ech-ushkya.

All that dirty river water ran into the once-beautiful ocean and soon the dragons and sea serpents were complaining, the mermaids and nereids were unhappy, and the banik were very angry and starting to talk about the need to do something about the mess.

Many of the human people began to protest the growing destruction, but the machines and the people who owned them were not in a mood to listen. They built factories which spewed streams of filthy smoke into the once-clear sky, and the birds began to fly away, looking for a clean place in which to raise their children.

Of course, the more factories and machines there were, the more coal the owners needed to run them and the more ore to build new places and parts; that meant that more and more miners had to go down into the ground and dig tunnels looking for what was needed. The bogeys and the boogies, the dwarfs and gnomes, the goblins and knockers were disturbed, and when the hammering and banging, drilling and exploding just got worse and worse, some of the underground people became quite upset. That is probably where the goblins and hobgoblins got their bad tempers.

The earth, the sky, the water, and the underground were all attacked in a most dishonourable way, and the lives of the people began to suffer. Little people and human people alike were much less happy than they had been, and some of them were even unhappy.

Human people worked long hard hours for little pay, and their children were always hungry because the gardens no longer flourished and the orchards no longer provided bountiful harvests. The houses in which they lived were small, and always cold in the winter, and the factories just kept spewing black smoke into the sky. And because there was so little food for the children, the human people stopped putting out food for the little people. They stopped putting out milk and cheese for the sidhe and the fairies, for the pixies, the piskies, and the dear goolyguys.

The children tried to feed the magic ones, but the children had almost nothing at all of their own, and so often the only thing the children could do was sing songs to let the sprites and spirits know that they had not been forgotten.

Everybody was very sad.

Then the parents heard there was a land far away

where there were no greedy people controlling all the land, and where the air was not polluted nor the water poisoned. A land that had everything anybody could ever want or need; fish to catch, berries to pick, fruit growing on healthy trees, and land to farm.

That was all anybody needed to hear!

Mothers began washing, mending and packing clothes, and fathers began hammering nails into boards to make boxes to ship the few things the people had. Grandfathers cleaned their tools and wrapped them carefully. Grandmothers checked to make sure the needles and threads and wool and scissors were carefully tucked in the sewing baskets.

The dishes were washed, dried, and packed in the boxes, with a layer of sheets on the bottom and a layer of blankets on top so none of the cups, saucers, or plates would be broken in the move. Each kettle was scrubbed and scoured, then wrapped in an uncle's heavy sweater and packed in the box. The teapot, the precious teapot in each home was washed, dried, then wrapped in the warm quilt and placed carefully in with the other things.

When everything was packed except the clothes they were wearing and one clean pair of socks for each, the people began to nail the lids on the boxes.

And suddenly, outside, all the bells began to ring! Big bells and little bells, medium-sized bells and cow bells, bells in church spires and bells over barn doors, bells, bells, bells, ringing wildly.

The children ran outside to see what was going on and the parents and grandparents, the aunts, uncles, and cousins ran after them.

That's when the magic people made their move! They came in through the windows, they came down the chimney, they came from behind the wood box. They came in under the crack of the back door, and in through the still-open front door. They came from the roof and they came from the drain spouts, they came from under the front porch and they came from under the back stairs.

They came up from the garden and down out of the trees, they came from the stores and the churches, they came from the street gratings and from under rocks, stones and pebbles, they came from the cracks in the mortar around the bricks and they came rushing all-in-a-dither from the back lane with their braces dangling and their socks only half pulled up, and two of them showed up with their shoes in their hands because they hadn't had time to put them on.

And they all jumped into the boxes to hide in, with, and among the treasures the people were taking with them to the new land.

Nobody was leaving any magic people behind, they said!

Nobody is leaving the adh seidh or the bain sidhe or the kelpies or the goblins or the gremlins or the bodach or the bendith y mamau, or the bogles or the cluricauns or the dwarfs or the elves or the fairies or the fauns or the grain guardians or any of the magic people!

They crept and slithered and writhed and cuddled down in the boxes full of belongings. Some of them curled up inside the cups and made themselves at home, others lay under saucer rims and still others set up housekeeping under and among the plates. Small ones found themselves very comfortable in the spoons, while larger ones preferred bowls and jars. Several families went down the spout of the kettle and while it was a little bit dark, it was very cozy and comfortable, thank you. The luckiest ones went into the teapot and tucked their babies in and told them hush, now, time to go to sleep.

Nobody could find any reason for the bells to be ringing. When the magic people who were in charge of the noise got the signal to hurry, they left off ringing the bells and raced to take their places in the big packing crates, so the bells fell silent. The people waited, asking each other questions nobody could answer. Questions like "Why are the bells ringing?" and "Does anybody know what's going on?"

Nobody knew why the bells were ringing and nobody knew what was going on, so finally the children headed back inside the houses, and the mothers and fathers, grandmothers and grandfathers, aunts, uncles, and cousins followed them.

And the last boards were nailed into place. The packing crates were shut.

Then the crates were lifted onto wagons and taken through the villages and towns, down roads and highways, down lanes and streets, to the city, then taken through the city to the docks where they were taken off the wagons and piled on top of big nets. When the nets were full, they were pulled shut and a big ring on top of the net was lifted to meet a huge hook coming from the sky. The skyhook fit through the ring and then, with a great deal of huffing and puffing and heaving and hauling and plenty of shouting, the nets were lifted from the dock and swung through the air.

Life for the magic people was not very nice! They had been bounced and jounced, they had been jiggled and joggled, they had been thumped and bumped, and now they were being swung aloft and swayed back and forth.

Then the nets were lowered into the hold of the ship. The skyhook was removed, the ring dropped, the net opened, and workers began to stack the packing crates in their proper place. And once again, the fairies and sprites, the goolyguys and the sidhe were lifted, moved, bumped, knocked, banged, and plunked. Some of them bruised their ankles and knees, others bruised fingers and toes. One or two bruised elbows and three very unfortunate silkies banged funnybones, and banged funnybones are never any fun!

But the magic people were determined, and the magic people were brave. Mothers kissed bruised fingers to make them better and fathers rubbed sore shins to help take the ouches away. Grandmothers cuddled frightened little ones and grandfathers settled themselves down with babies and toddlers cradled close and began to softly sing all those songs which have always made little ones feel better. Tears dried and frowns vanished. Before long, the little magic ones fell asleep, some of them sucking thumbs and others clinging to their favourite blanket or quilt.

The people walked up a gangway and on to the ship, then made their way to the place where they were to stay during the long trip.

It wasn't very nice. Only the rich people could afford tickets which entitled them to private or semi-private staterooms. The poor people had to make do with what they had. But they were used to hardship. They were used to scarce food. They knew their discomforts would not last forever.

And they had their music!

One young woman had a fiddle, and another young woman had a drum. Someone had a whistle and someone else had a squeeze-box. Grandmothers pulled kitchen spoons from where they had hidden them in apron pockets, held the handles between their fingers, and clattered the bowls of the spoons together rhythmically. Grandfathers pulled rib bones from their pockets and clattered them the same way the grandmothers played the spoons. Two men had jaw harps, a teenaged boy had a mouth organ, and every family had someone who could play the guitar, mandolin, banjo, or at least the sole of someone's shoes.

Cousins danced with aunties, children danced with grandparents, and when they were all too tired to sing, play, or dance any more, they lay down on the floor and went to sleep.

Day after day after day after day the people suffered and day after day after day after day they met their suffering with song and bravery. Day after day after day after day the ship moved across the great heaving sea, closer, ever closer to the new land.

"Avalon," said the grandparents, "used to be called Ynys yr Afallon, which meant 'Island of Apples.' It is a place of green meadows and flowers, a place where apple trees blossom year-round and the buzzing of bees fills the air. With the apple trees blooming all year, the bees have all the pollen and nectar they need to make honey, so the bees are happy and never sting, and any time anyone wants honey, they have only to go to the beehives with a container. The honey will drip from the overflowing hive and fill the jar or the pot or the pitcher. Apples ripen while there are still blossoms on the boughs, and the sound of sweet music is heard whenever a person wants to hear it."

"Avalon," said the aunts and uncles, "is a place where the rain falls at night when everyone is asleep, so the grass is always green and the flowers are always blooming, but nobody ever gets wet or cold or muddy. There are fish in the streams and rivers, and any time a person wants to eat fish, he or she has only to go to the bank of the stream and put a basket on the grass. Then that person sings a song, and the fish leap from the water into the basket, and in the leaping, they go from being raw to being cooked your favourite way. If you want a drink of milk, you have only to leave the milk jug on the top step at night, and when you get up in the morning the jug is full. At least once a day, if your kitchen is clean and your table tidy, suddenly, by magic, there will be a loaf of bread and a nice sweet cake."

"Avalon," said the children, "is a place where you can play all day without ever having to worry about anything. Avalon is a place where you are always warm and dry, unless you're swimming, and then you're warm and wet. You have lots of food and a soft bed to sleep in, and nobody ever has to do without the things they need."

In the storage hold where the packing crates and home-made boxes and trunks were stored, the magic people waited, snuggled down in their hidey-holes and peeky-places. They cuddled their babies and smooched their children, they whispered secrets and told jokes, they tickled tiny toes, and sang magic songs, and waited.

Then, finally, oh joy oh joy, the big boat landed at the dock! The people packed their few things, trooped down the gangway, and stood looking around them.

"Is this Avalon?" the children asked.

"Where are the apple trees?"

"Where is the music?"

"Where is the honey?"

"Where are the streams full of fish?"

They saw the dock, they saw wharves and piers, they saw ships with sails and other ships with stacks belching black smoke. They saw stevedores and navvies, they saw huge cranes unloading nets full of boxes and suitcases. They saw many many things, but they did not see green grass or blossoming apple trees, they did not see flowers or honey bees, they did not see birds flying in the air and they did not see fish eager to be eaten.

"No," said the grandparents, "this is not Avalon."

The children were disappointed but they put their best faces on and picked up their little karazinkas and trudged after the parents, the aunties and uncles, the older cousins, and the grandparents. Past the warehouses and storage sheds, past the working stevedores and toiling navvies, past the nets and boxes, past the cranes and the packing crates, down the street and across the avenue.

And there, the already travel-weary people climbed on to a train!

They sat in the train and waited for their boxes and packing cases, their steamer trunks and home-made crates to be unloaded from the ship, put on wagons or trucks, and taken to the station where they were loaded into freight cars.

Once again the magic people were bumped and jostled, shaken and rattled, turned upside down, and generally jiggled. One of the teapots slipped and would have banged against the stew pot and been smashed into shards but the magic ones intervened. The goolyguys, the faithful, warm-hearted, helpful little goolyguy dove bravely across the space to reach out and grab the handle.

The goolyguy is very slender, with huge round dark eyes and long, thin hands and fingers with little blunt-tipped pads on the ends. She is very shy, and is seldom seen because she comes out mostly at night. Her hair is jet black and sometimes it is curly, sometimes it is straight, depending on what kind of hair her mother and father had. Straight or curly, her hair grows in every direction at the same time, bushing out from her head in a most wonderful wild way. Goolyguys are very good with animals and often live in barns or stables.

What the people can't get done during the day, the

goolyguy comes out to do at night. She will not live where the people are lazy, however; the goolyguy will not do all the work while people sit around playing cards and wasting time. The goolyguy only lives where people are willing to do their share and then some.

With her long, thin hands and her slender, blunt-tipped fingers, the goolyguy puts tools back where they belong. She picks up milk pails and puts them back on their nails when the cats have knocked them off. She chases the weasels away from the chicken house. She weeds the garden and makes sure the night dew washes clean the faces of the flowers and plants.

And all she asks is that from time to time a bowl of milk or a piece of cheese or a slice of apple or maybe a piece of home-made buttered bread be left on the porch for her. Or for him if it happens to be a boy goolyguy.

And sometimes, when the teapot is about to be smashed to smithereens in the packing crate, the goolyguy dives like a hero or a hera and grabs the handle, and it doesn't even matter that the grandmother might never know who it was who saved her all-time most favourite teapot. For the goolyguy, just doing a good job is what is important.

When all the crates and boxes were stacked in place, the train began to huff and puff and chuff and then the whistle blew toot-toot rooty-tooty. Black smoke belched from the stack and white steam gushed from around the wheels. All the children grabbed for the big cousins, the aunts and uncles, the mothers and fathers, the grandmothers and grandfathers. The big bell rang ding-dong cling-clong ring-a-ding-a-boing boing.

And the train began to move.

"Listen," said a grandmother, "listen to what the train is saying!"

"All I heard," sniffled a very frightened little boy, "all

I hear is chunga-chunga chunga-chunga..."

"No," the grandmother smiled. "No, listen. A-va-lon...A-va-lon...Avalon, Avalon, avalonavalon, avalonavalonavalon... listen and you'll hear it, avalon avalon... we're going to Avalon...."

The children listened. They heard rickety-tickety and clickety-clackety, they heard chug-a-chug, they heard huffa-huffa and they heard puffa-puffa, they heard wheels clattering and rails bouncing, they heard things jingle and jangle, they heard bumps and bangs and then—

"I hear it!" said the small boy, no longer frightened. "I hear it! A-va-lon, A-va-lon, we're going to Avalon..."

And all the children rushed to open the windows and poke out their heads so they could hear better.

Blond hair and brown hair and black hair, short hair and long hair, straight hair and curly hair, even red hair blew in the breeze of the train's passing.

"A-va-lon," the children shouted, "we're going to Avalon!"

Day after day after day after day the train chugged and huffed from the east to the west. The children got very very weary. There was no running around outside, no playing ball, no playing soccer, no anything at all except maybe a little bit of hide'n'seek, but there aren't many places to hide on a moving train and anyway everybody had to be very careful not to step on anybody else's toes.

Day after day after day, and a person sure can get sick and tired of nothing to eat but cheese sandwiches, and nothing to drink but water! When one family used up the last of their bread and cheese, the other families shared with them. But every day someone else ran out of food, and pretty soon all the people were starting to feel very very hungry. And just when nobody had any food left, the train stopped....

"Quickly!" the oldest grandmother cried. "Quickly! Everybody dig deep for those last few pennies. Alice and Jeremy, you are the fastest runners. Take the money and go into town and buy as much bread and cheese as you can! David and Daniel and Sarah, you are the strongest. Follow them and help carry it back! Hurry now, hurry!"

Alice and Jeremy took the money and raced from the train lickety-split, with David, Daniel, and Sarah following. Away from the train, down the street to the bread and cheese shop.

"Bread," puffed Alice.

"Cheese," panted Jeremy.

"Bread and cheese," they managed to explain, putting all the money on the counter.

The lady brought bread and cheese, loaves and wheels and pieces and slices.

"I'll help you," she laughed, "or you'll never get back before the train leaves!"

Lickety-split left-foot-right-foot, arms loaded with loaves of bread and rounds of cheese, the children hurried back to the train, helped by the lady from the bread and cheese store.

Meanwhile, the train men and women filled the tanks with water, unhitched the empty fuel cars, and hitched up the full ones. The stokers shovelled coal into the big furnace and the fire flared and heated the water in the tank, making steam to drive the engine faster and faster.

Just in time, the children returned with the bread and cheese. They raced up the little metal steps, passing bread and cheese to the people on the train.

"Catch!" the lady from the store called, and she threw loaves to the children who passed them to the big cousins who passed them to the parents, the aunts and uncles, the grandmothers and grandfathers.

"Don't forget this!" the lady called, tossing wheels of cheese and rounds of cheese and even a few slices of cheese.

"Thank you!" the children called and waved.

"Ooooooooops!!" And they all laughed as the lady threw the last small round of cheese and it missed the eagerly reaching hands and landed, instead, in a freight car!

"Ooooooooops!!" the lady called. "Sorry!"

But the magic people weren't sorry! Even though they are magic, and even though they can do wonderful things, the little people cannot make cheese. They can make magic cakes out of barley, cakes that are so magic a person can eat her or his fill and still the barley cake will not be all eaten. People have been known to live off one magic barley cake for weeks and even months without reducing the size of that barley cake.

But the magic people cannot make cheese. And oh, they do love cheese!

A pisky or a pixie would rather have a nice piece of cheese than a strawberry shortcake! An elf would rather have cheese than candy! A goblin, hobgoblin, and a bogle would all rather have cheese than anything else in the world, even peaches or grapes. And a goolyguy... well, a goolyguy positively yearns for cheese and never gets enough.

So the magic people came from their hidey-holes, nooks, crannies, and sneak-spots and danced around the cheese. All the magic people, the leprechauns and the bogeys and the pukas and the pookys and the trolls and the sidhe and all the rest of them, celebrated happily. Then they say down and very generously, with no argument or blether, shared the cheese, making certain the littlest ones got fed first.

The people on the train shared their bread and

cheese too. Then, bellies full for the first time in days and days, they listened as the young woman played the fiddle and the other musicians accompanied her on their instruments. One old grandmother got up and showed the children a new dance step, and the children were busy the rest of the day practising it and showing each other how well they could do it.

"Oh, happy day," they sang. "Oh, happy day!"

The train moved along the tracks day after day and night after night. The children saw miles and miles and miles and miles and miles and still more miles of flat grassland.

"Is this Avalon?" asked the littlest ones.

"There are no apple trees," said an older one. "This is not Avalon!"

They saw animals such as they had never seen in what they were already calling the Old Country. They saw buffalo and antelope, they saw wolves and coyotes, they saw deer and they saw wild horses. They saw hawks and eagles, they saw falcons and jays, and they saw hundreds and hundreds of prairie dogs.

And when they had seen just about as much of the prairies as they ever wanted to see... MOUNTAINS!! Far in the distance, reaching for the sky, tipped with snow and ice, waiting and beckoning, mountains, mountains, mountains!

They were so awed and so astounded nobody could say anything at all. All day the train chugged and puffed, huffed and hauled up, up, up, up, up, ever upward, past trees and rocks, past creeks and rivers, up and up, and up, up, up, until nobody believed they could get very much higher than this.

"Look," said a young boy. "Look. No matter how high we are, the hawks are flying higher!"

"Yes!" said a small girl. "And look at the eagles, too!

They are 'way, 'way, 'way up there!"

Up and up and up they went, past waterfalls and the first snow patches, up and up and up and then—

"Oh, momma, LOOK AT THAT!" a little girl screeched. "Oh look, look, look-look-look!"

They all rushed to the windows and stared in amazement. And the mountain goats stared back, not the least bit amazed, for they had seen lots and lots of trains with lots and lots of thunderstruck people staring out the windows.

"Oh, oh, oh!!" the children breathed, unable to utter one single solitary word that could even begin to explain what it was they were feeling. "Oh, oh, oh!"

And then they were at the top of the mountain pass, and the tracks were shining ahead of them, down, down, down, down, down, past the snow and ice, past the tip-top peaks hidden by cloud and mist, down, down, down, all day and all night. Down, down, following streams and rivers, following the shining twin tracks, down, down, down. And when the moon and stars came out, the children were still peering out the little train windows trying to see where it was they were going.

"Now, now," said the grandmothers, "if you fall asleep at the window you'll wake up with a crick in your neck. Come, now, and lie down here on the floor, and Granny will wrap you warm in your own nice jacket and sing you a song."

"But—" yawned the children. "But I want to see!"

"You'll see better after a nice sleep," the grandmothers promised. "There, now, just close your eyes and go to sleep...."

When the children were asleep, the big cousins went to sleep. Then the aunties and uncles, then the mothers and fathers. Finally, when everyone else was asleep, the grandmothers and grandfathers closed their tired old wrinkled eyelids over their tired old eyes and they, too, went to sleep.

"LOOK! LOOK LOOK LOOK!!" screeched a little girl.

Everybody jerked awake and raced to the windows.

"Oh, look! Oh! Oh!"

"Oh," they said, and there was nothing else to say, just "oh."

"But what IS it?" asked a little boy with curly red hair. "What is it, Granny?"

"The ocean," Granny said.

The waves lapped at the sand and rock shoreline, great green trees marched to the very lip of the sea, and massive bare rocks leapt up to meet the sky. The twin tracks moved as close to the marvel as was safe, and the children all stared round-eyed and open-mouthed at the beauty spread out before them.

They saw arbutus trees bent and twisted by the wind, growing in places you wouldn't think any tree could survive. They saw cedar trees with enormous outstretching uplifting boughs. They saw fir trees and maple trees, alder trees and wild cherry trees, hemlock and spruce and willow trees. They saw seagulls and osprey, they saw kingfishers and herons, they saw sandpipers and they saw mergansers. They saw sand and rocks, they saw barnacles and oysters clinging to the boulders and cliffs, they saw driftwood and they saw fish jumping into the air and splashing back into the water.

"Oh!" they breathed. "Oh, oh, oh!"

When the train finally stopped, the people got off and stood together for comfort, not at all sure where they were or what they were supposed to do. The freight cars were unloaded and the boxes and crates were stacked where the people could find their own things, and then the train chug-a-chugged away and the children, the older cousins, the parents, and aunts and uncles, the grandmothers and grandfathers were alone beside the tracks in a country none of them had ever seen before, and few had heard of or even imagined.

"Is this Avalon?" asked a little voice.

Nobody knew whether this was Avalon or not. But you can't spend all your life standing around doing nothing. You can't spend all your life standing by the tracks with your suitcases, steamer trunks, and packing crates jumbled at your feet, wondering. And so the people who had left the Old Country for the New Country picked up their belongings and headed away from the tracks.

Big strong uncles managed to balance packing crates on their broad shoulders, and grown cousins lifted trunks and suitcases. Aunties cut strong poles and tied them to heavy boxes, then, an auntie-at-either-end, they lifted the poles to their shoulders and set off with the load shared by two.

Grandparents lifted bundles and parents lifted suitcases and children picked up karazinkas and all trudged off bravely.

They walked through forest groves and through sunlit glades, they walked past beautiful big clumps of fern and past enormous trees whose trunks and boles were sheathed in soft moss. They walked under outspread boughs and strong branches, they walked beside crystal-clear streams and sparkling lakes.

A little boy trudged to the bank of the stream and set his karazinka on the ground. He took off his cap and began to sing. Tra-la-la tra-la-la tra-la-la.

"No fish," he mourned. "No fish jumped out all cooked and ready to eat! This is not Avalon. This is just someplace or other like any place anywhere else. I thought we were going to Avalon. That's what I thought!"

He picked up his karazinka and followed the others.

"They told me Avalon," he insisted. "That's what they told me!"

They walked across a meadow of long green grass where lupins and snapdragons grew, every colour a person could imagine was there, and bumbly bees with big fuzzy bums moved from flower to flower collecting pollen.

"It might not be Avalon," a little girl said, "but it is beautiful!"

"They told me Avalon," the little boy insisted. "I rode on a boat for days and days and then I rode on a train for days and days. I ate bread and cheese and cheese and bread and waited for days and days because they said Avalon. But when I sang for a fish. . . nothing!"

"I don't care," the little girl said, "I like it. I like the flowers and I like the ferns and I like the birds and I particularly like the big-bummed bumbly bees."

"It's still not Avalon," the little boy said. "It is the most beautiful place I have ever seen, and the flowers are lovely and the water is clean and I like the bumbly bees but it is not Avalon. They shouldn't have said Avalon if they didn't mean Avalon."

"But didn't it make you feel happier to hear about Avalon?" someone else asked.

"They said Avalon," the little boy said firmly. That's what they said. Yes, it made me feel better. So what? Is this Avalon? No, it is not!"

"I am going to ask my mother and father to build our house here," the girl said. "I don't care if it isn't Avalon, it's wonderful!" And she hurried to her parents and tugged at their sleeves. "Could we build a house here?" she asked. "We could have a garden, and we could have chickens, and we could have ducks to swim in the pond, and maybe even berries from those bushes. . ."

Her mother and father looked around them. They saw the open field, the bright sunshine, the trees bordering the clearing and the stream running through it. And they sat down, smiling.

"It isn't Avalon," the little boy said.

One by one the families found the places they liked best. Some people wanted to live by the pond, some wanted to live by the stream, some liked it better in the cool green woods and some wanted to live where they could see and hear the ocean. One by one they chose their places, and then everybody pitched in to help everybody else build their houses. And the grandparents got their houses built first.

Trees were cut down and made into walls and floors, window frames and roofs, front steps and back steps and doors. Other trees were turned into tables and chairs, and still other trees were turned into beds and benches. First one house, then another, then a third and then a fourth. Chicken coops and cow byres, duck sheds and wood sheds, barns and stables, and even doghouses were built.

And once everybody had a house, it was time to unpack all the things they had brought from the Old Country and put them away, to turn the houses into homes. The fathers and uncles and big cousins pried the nailed-down planks off the packing crates. They unpacked the top layer of quilts and blankets to make up the beds.

And—zip!—out jumped the magic people who had been hiding there all that long long time. They came out of the stitching in the quilts, and from the hems of the sheets. They came from inside the pillows and from the embroidery on the pillow slips. They came from inside cups and bowls, they came from where they had snuggled down in spoons and they even came pouring out the spouts of kettles and teapots! The adh seidh and the bain sidhe and the kelpies, and the goblins and the gremlins and the bodach and the bendith y mamau, and the cluricauns and the lepre-chauns and the dwarfs and the elves and the fairies and the fauns and the grain guardians and, of course, the goolyguys. Out came the piskies, and out came the pixies and the pookas and the pukas. Out came the silkies and out came the sealkies, and out came the trolls and the brownies.

With their babies tucked under their arms and their children riding on their backs, the magic ones raced happily for the New Country. The wood sprites cheered when they saw the seemingly endless forests of huge happy trees, and the water sprites gurgles with joy when they saw the creeks, streams, rivers, ponds, and lakes. The flower fairies sang and raced for the lupin, the snapdragons, the columbines, and the day lilies, and the air was filled with the sound of their laughter.

The goolyguy raced for the forest, laughing happily, glad to be able to fully stretch her long arms and long, slender legs. Another goolyguy capered in the dappled shade of the forest, waving his fingers and laughing because he had been cramped and uncomfortable for so long.

"Free free free!" the goolyguys cheered. "Free free fr—" They stopped, their big soft round dark eyes widening with surprise and maybe even the first flutter of fear...

Floating in mid-air, dancing like dust motes in the sunlight, shimmering and gleaming and tinkling like teeny-weeny itsy-bitsy silver bells, were hundreds, maybe thousands of creatures nobody had ever seen in their long magical lives. Little bright shining silvery bubbles, tinkling like bells, and inside each of the bubbles, a little figure.

For all the hundreds and thousands and maybe even millions of years that the little people had lived in the

Old Country, for all that long long time and all their long long lives, they had never ever—not one single time—even suspected that there could be anything at all like these little bubbles. They almost ran away but they didn't know where they were so they certainly didn't know where to go.

And the goolyguys are always very brave.

They stood, waiting to see what these bright bubbles were. They stood, listening to the tinkling sounds from the dancing silvery globes. And the goolyguys realized the tinkling sounds were the sounds of voices, and the sounds of laughter. They dared move closer, they dared conquer their fear and step up carefully to the dancing orbs.

That's when they saw the Stlalacum for the first time. Inside each globe was a tiny figure dressed in a kilt or a skirt of woven cedar bark, wearing a tiny dance cape decorated with bits of abalone shell and mother-of-pearl, with dentalia shell and polished mussel shell, with hummingbird feathers and red-shafted flicker feathers, with blue jay feathers and magical stones with holes in them. The goolyguys looked at each other, then looked at the Stlalacum and smiled. The New Country had magic people of its own!

The Stlalacum introduced the goolyguys to other magic people, to the stick people and the rock people, to the breeze people and the wind people, to the river people and the spindrift people, to the sand people and the little round-faced people who live in the huckleberry bushes and the little black-faced people who live in the blackberry bushes. The goolyguys met the little women who live in the daisy fields and the little yellow-faced people who live in the dandelions. The kelpies, which can appear as either humans or horses, and who live in rivers or streams, met the water-walking people of the new land, and the mermaids and

mermen who had raced for the ocean met Flood Tide
Woman and Ebb Tide Woman and the spindrift people.
The nixies, who live in fresh water, met the shy fresh
water people, and the nymphs and nyads who live in
trees met the forest dwelling people. The grain
guardians met the protectors of the grass and the
guardians of the forest.

For every magic person from the Old Country, there
was a magic person from the new land, and if they
looked different, so what, there was room for all and
no need for fear or distrust.

The underground people moved aside to make room
for the trolls and goblins, and the tree spirits shoved
over to allow the nymphs and sprites plenty of room.
Arbutus Mother bent herself just a little bit more and
the woodland spirits said thank you very much and set
up their housekeeping. Cedar Woman sighed a welcome and Alder Mother gladly made room for the
hawthorne spirit. The elderberry dwellers of the new
land gasped with joy when they realized that the old
lady of the elder groves had come with the other magic
people from the Old Country. The little old lady of the
elder groves is seldom seen by humans, and those few
who have seen her have seen her only at harvest time.
She is tiny, and her dress is either as black as black
elderberry or as deep red as red elderberry. Her cap
and shawl are as white and lacy as elderberry flowers
and she has a cane or a crutch made from elder wood.

The people unpacked their tools and began to dig
and plant their gardens. The goolyguys went out every
night to help with the weeding. The children, who have
never broken faith with the magic ones, left pieces of
cheese and nice slices of buttered bread.

The willing worker people watched as the goolyguys
picked weeds, then sat on the steps of the houses and
feasted on what the children had left for them. And

when the willing worker people came forward in the moonlight to see just what was going on anyway, the goolyguys shared the treats with them. The willing worker people had never tasted milk or cheese or bread or butter before, and they liked it very much! They moved into the gardens to help the goolyguy with the weeding and the watering and the protecting of the plants.

And the willing worker people took the goolyguy with them to the villages of the good people, the civilized people, the coast people, the gentle people, and showed the goolyguy how to ensure that the fish lines were in good repair and the dugouts were properly cared for. And the goolyguys, for the first time in all history, tasted the food of the original people in the new land. They tasted a wonderful kind of bread called scouse and they tasted oolichan oil. They tasted smoked fish and they tasted the little yellow potato which has always grown on the coast.

The children of the original people looked out of their longhouses and saw a goolyguy for the first time, then looked at each other with surprise-widened eyes and wondered what the goolyguy could possibly be. But they saw the willing worker spirits with the goolyguy and decided whatever the strange-looking new spirits were, they were not bad ones.

The children of the newcomers looked out their windows and saw the willing worker people with the goolyguys, picking weeds in the gardens, and they had no idea what it was they were seeing. But if the little people in the woven cedar bark kilts, capes, and conical hats were friends of the goolyguys, the children knew they were good little people, even if they were strangers.

And one day, the little boy who had tried to sing a fish out of the stream went for a walk. He walked across the flower-studded meadow and through the fringe of forest to the stream, then up the stream to where he knew there was a beautiful deep pool at the bottom of a waterfall.

But when he stepped from the forest shade, he froze in his tracks. Standing by the pool, wearing a woven cedar bark kilt, was a boy who was staring in disbelief at the boy in homespun pants and shirt.

The two children stared at each other, and each one knew the other was scared stiff. So each one tried to show the other there was nothing to be afraid of, and smiled, and held out his hand. In no time flat, both boys were checking the fish traps the dark-skinned boy had set in the pond. And in less time than it would take to tell of it, a friendship was formed. The dark-skinned boy gave fresh trout to the newcomer, to take home and share with his family.

After supper, the newcomers all walked along the shore to the village of the good people. All the magic people of the two countries watched as the human people met each other. And while the adults stood around not knowing what to say or how to say it, what to do or how to do it, the children moved forward.

And then the young woman began to play the fiddle, and a young man began to play a concertina. One person grabbed a drum and another grabbed up a flute. Spoons were clattered, shoes were slapped, hands clapped, fingers snapped, rattles rattled and people began to dance.

In the forest all the forest people danced and in the meadow the meadow people danced. Out on the waves the sea people danced and the breeze people celebrated by coming down to blow everybody's hair every which way.

"Avalon," some of the people sang, "Avalon."

"Home," other people sang. "Home home home."

# NOTES ON THE MAGIC ONES

**BANIKS** live near water. They are particularly fond of saunas and sweat-houses, but are also found in outdoor hot pools, flitting in the thick steam. You seldom see the banik, but sometimes you can feel a light touch on your skin. If she touches you softly it is a sign of good luck coming your way, but if she scratches you, you are being warned of bad luck to come.

**BLACK DOGS.** Sometimes people see a dog walking with them, a black dog which looks like a labrador retriever, but the dog makes no sound. You can't hear its breathing or its nails clicking on the sidewalk. If you speak to it, it ignores you. Some people feel frightened of the dog, but they are usually the kind of people who are afraid of everything. The black dog can bring very good luck to people who are willing to walk with it and who do not run away; after all, it is just a black dog, and it has never bitten anyone, so why be afraid just because it is silent?

The **BODACH** looks like a shrivelled-up little old bald-headed man. He lives in the chimney during the day and comes out at night. The bodach is the one who listens to see if little kids are going to bed with no fuss; if they do, the bodach leaves them alone. If they fuss and cry and snivel and want to stay up for just one more program, please Mum please, then the bodach comes out while they're asleep and pulls their noses, tweaks their ears, and ties their hair in knots so it hurts to brush it the next day. Sometimes, if the child has been really awful, the bodach will open his eyelids, peer into his eyes, and give him awful nightmares. You can keep the bodach away by putting some salt in the stove at night before you go to bed. This makes him so thirsty he spends the whole night drinking water and leaving you alone.

**BOGEYS** or **BOOGIES** or **BOGEYMEN** live underground or in darkness, so they are found in basements or closets or barns, or sometimes under logs or in hollow trees. Bogeys are particularly fond of the stuff people no longer use but refuse to throw away, so they like garages, attics, and old suitcases. Junk shops, antique shops, and filing cabinets are good places to look for them. Sometimes bogeys play tricks: they pull off your covers on a cold night, or they sneak up and blow cold breath on the back of your neck. They move around mostly at night, and you lie in bed and hear creakings and groanings and you get scared and then someone says, "Oh, it's just the house settling." It isn't the house settling, it's the silly bogeys moving around looking for junk.

**BOGLES,** like bogeys, enjoy living where there is lots of old stuff. A good way to tell whether a bogle is there or not is to find a knothole and look through it. If there's a bogle on the other side, you'll get a quick gleam of his eye before he has time to pull away and hide. Cracks in the wooden wall are almost as good as knotholes, but not quite.

**BOGGARTS.** Sometimes mistaken for brownies, boggarts are not as helpful, mainly because they are clumsy and most of the things they try to do wind up becoming inexplicable accidents. When a boggart tries to herd the cows home, the cows panic and take off in all directions, when the boggart tries to get the chickens to go back to the hen house to roost, the chickens fly off into the trees. Boggarts tip over the milk, make dogs yap for no known reason, make the taps drip and the kettle boil dry. Sometimes a baby will start to cry and nothing anybody does will stop the crying. That baby has been frightened by a boggart.

**BROWNIES** are earth spirits who originated in Scotland. Very cheerful and helpful, they can be seen only by happy, cheerful people, and they are the proof that you do not have to be beautiful to be nice! They are small, usually hairy, with little pinholes for nostrils and no nose at all. They enjoy playing with children, and they are the ones who tell the cows when it is time to start for home, the ones who keep the chickens heading back to roost at night. Some people put gifts out for the brownies, to say thank you, but the brownies never take the food. They leave it for other little folk. Brownies only want to be liked, and to make others as happy as they are. Brownies are also the ones who run around trying to undo the mischief done by goblins.

**CLURICAUNS** live in cellars and basements and under barns and houses. They wear breeches, stockings, white shirts, aprons, silver-buckled shoes, and little red pointy caps. They particularly like wine cellars, breweries and wineries, hotels, inns and restaurants. In a good restaurant or inn, the cluricaun watches what the people are doing, sings and dances in the shadows, and nibbles happily from the food in the kitchen. In bad restaurants, he devours food, swills liquor, and even takes things from some people and gives them to others, so that eventually the bad restaurant or inn will go broke and have to close. A cluricaun is a very nasty drunk, breaking bottles and glasses, keeping everyone awake as he lurches around singing off-key and knocking over furniture, pulling the cat's tail, making the dogs bark, and, because he likes to swing from the clock weights when he is drunk, the people in the house are apt to be late for work. The only way to get rid of a drunken cluricaun is to have everyone in the house stop drinking. Very shortly, the cluricaun will leave and go look for some other place where he can get at the booze. There seems to be no record of female cluricauns.

**DRYADS** are forest-dwelling nymphs, shy like all nymphs but especially afraid of humans because we will insist on cutting down trees.

**DWARFS** are sometimes confused with gnomes, which are perfectly formed. Dwarfs have deformed, twisted bodies, oversized heads, and unpleasant faces. There are male and female dwarfs, and child dwarfs have been seen. They live underground most of the time, but sometimes show up to help celebrate birthdays and other anniversaries. Dwarfs are seen by humans in the wintertime, when they go into houses to get warm. The colder the winter, the more dwarfs will appear. If dwarfs come into your house and start to have a party, you must not join in unless you are invited. If you are invited and you refuse, the dwarfs will be insulted and bring you bad luck. If, however, you are invited to join the party and you can sing or tap-dance, the dwarfs will be charmed and you will have good luck for seven years. Dwarfs are usually employed as miners but are equally skilled as blacksmiths, ironmongers, and makers of metal jewellery. Dwarfs made the ring Odin gave his wife as a present. In the mines, if a human miner meets a dwarf, he is supposed to doff his hat, nod greeting, then open his lunch box and invite the dwarf to eat whatever he wants. If the miner doesn't have his lunch kit with him, he should turn his pockets inside out; sometimes dwarfs will take a penny or a nickel which they may make into a ring or other piece of jewellery. Meeting a dwarf in a mine is considered good luck—the dwarfs often lead the miners to the motherlode.

**ECH-USHKYAS.** Like kelpies, the water horse of the rivers, the ech-ushkya is the water horse of the lakes. But the ech-ushkya is a people-eater. Anyone who climbs on its back is unable to get off it again. The ech-ushkya runs into the lake, the person drowns, and the ech-ushkya eats him.

**ELVES** live in the woods. They are like tiny humans, but much better looking and much much more graceful. They are very clever, can predict the future, and spend most of their time dancing and singing. Nobody really understands elves, who are sometimes very nice, sometimes quite nasty. There is no known protection against them. They come and go as whim takes them but seldom stay long in any one place. It does no good to leave food out for them because no one is quite sure what they eat.

**FAIRIES** or **FAERIES,** "the Little People," usually appear as miniature humans, and are capable of growing or shrinking. They seldom get any bigger than knee-high to a six-year-old child, but they can get small enough to pass through the eye of a needle. Fairies usually travel in a troupe, and can only be seen for small periods of time: if you blink, they are gone. Therefore, people who can stare without blinking get a better view than most people. Dogs and cats can see fairies better than humans can, and there is reason to believe song birds are very friendly with fairies. Their magic is known as "glamour," and is very very strong. If you should happen to find a rock with a hole in it, you can often use it as a spy-glass—look through it and you might see fairies dancing in the flowers, ferns, and grass on the other bank of the stream. It is foolish to cross the stream for a better look, however, because as soon as you move toward them they will disappear.

Fairies are ruled by the fairy queen (called Mab or sometimes Meg), whose family originated on the Faro Islands. Each troop is ruled by a sub-queen and a varying number of princesses.

Occasionally a fairy will marry a human male. The result is always tragic; fairies cannot cook or do housework, and they find human life incredibly boring. Fairies also have a different religion than humans have, and consider it punishment to have to go to human churches. Inevitably, the fairy returns to her troupe, especially if she has a baby, for as soon as the baby is born, the fairy returns and takes it with her to be raised as a fairy.

Fairies eat almost everything humans eat, but they do not like to work. Sometimes they raid human gardens. If a person willingly shares, they will bless the garden and cast a glamour to encourage it to grow.

Fairies can disguise themselves as humans and their glamour makes them appear human-sized. They often appear at parties and impress everyone immediately with their graceful dancing, their beautiful singing, and their absolute beauty. Long after the party is over, people talk of the glamorous stranger who attended and charmed everyone. You can sometimes spot them, however, because of the little human traits which fairies cannot imitate or perhaps don't notice. For example, they can only turn to the left when dancing, and are capable of eating an extraordinary amount of good food. Fairies are also incapable of telling fibs, so they say things which surprise or even shock people. "Lovely food, isn't it?" might well be answered with "Well, most of it is, but the casserole is awful!" Fairies have the gift of gab and can speak every known language. They can play almost every instrument and know the words to all the songs.

A **FAUN** has the legs, tail, mane, and ears of a deer, and the body and face of a handsome young man. Fauns play flutes and dance, and are no threat at all to humans. In fact a faun can be a benefit if it lives in your orchard because its flute attracts the honeybees who will then pollinate the fruit trees and generate a bumper crop. Fauns are especially fond of apple orchards.

**FOMORS.** The Fomors or Fomorians are a race of giant magical people who were the original inhabitants of Scotland, Ireland, and possibly Wales. These indigenous or native people have practically disappeared in the Old Country, though it is said that in Scotland there are many half-breed or quarter-breed Fomorians, and that is why some Scottish people are so tall and so strong.

181

**GNOMES** are small, seldom taller than three inches high, and come in all shapes, with every possible kind of facial feature. They usually look like humans. Gnomes are invariably good-natured. They cannot worry or be angry for more than three seconds, and they never forget the lessons of their own past history, so they do not make the same mistakes over and over again. Gnomes have learned how to live with and co-operate with everything that shares the earth. Only humans have ever been a problem to gnomes.

Gnomes originally lived underground, but all the mining and tunnelling with its attendant noise and explosions made the underground less welcoming, so the gnomes moved above ground to the darkly shaded old forest which used to cover the Old Country. However, humans started cutting down the forests, and the gnomes were again disturbed. They were very glad of the opportunity to leave the Old Country, and they always celebrate the anniversary of their family's arrival in the new world, but they mourn the repetition of past mistakes and are forever trying to educate humans by reminding us of what happens when you cut down the forests.

**GOBLINS** or **HOBGOBLINS** are very nasty. All you have to do is look at them and you know how nasty they can be. When a goblin laughs, the milk goes sour, the hens stop laying, and the bees swarm to get away from the sound. All a goblin seems to want to do is make bad luck, bring nightmares, and cause accidents. Goblins may well be as bad-tempered and nasty as they are because of the way humans have cut down the forests and polluted the rivers and dug tunnels in the earth where goblins used to live.

Hobgoblins are the nastiest of all the goblins

because they have moved into houses where they spend their lives tormenting people.

**GOOLYGUYS,** the name for both males and females, are tall, slender, hairy brown creatures with big round dark brown eyes and very very *very* long blunt-tipped fingers. They keep the weeds out of the garden, look after the trees in the orchard, care for the hens and the ducks, talk to the geese, and comfort the cows. A goolyguy cannot touch metal of any kind. Do not leave nails lying around on the ground; a goolyguy might step on one and even if the nail doesn't go in the goolyguy's foot, she will be burned. Old cans, bottle caps, etc., anything made of metal must be put away in case a baby goolyguy touches it and gets injured.

Goolyguys cannot tell lies or do harmful tricks. They really only want to be liked. They are enormously grateful if you leave some food out for them: fruit, cheese, milk, fresh bread. They also love pie, cake, cookies, and pudding, foods they cannot make by themselves because they would have to touch the stove, the cookie sheet, or the cooking pot.

Goolyguy babies make wonderful friends. Often a young human child will talk to a friend no one else can see or hear, and the adults will speak of the "invisible playmate" and laugh and say, "Such an imagination!" These adults have forgotten much more than they should have. The invisible playmate is probably a little goolyguy. Of course the goolyguy baby cannot play with metal toys, but they can play with wooden toys and they love rag dolls and stuffed teddy bears. Sometimes goolyguy babies like to sleep over with human children. When that happens, the mother goolyguy will spend the night sitting on the window sill keeping watch over the children.

**GRAIN GUARDIANS** come in various shapes and sizes depending on which of the grains or cereals they protect. The most important and respected of all magic people, the grain goddesses and gods cause the wheat, corn, flax, barley, etc., to grow and ripen and provide us with food. It is very important not to insult the grain guardians: if we waste what they provide, they will take it from us. And what would life be without breads, cake, or corn-on-the-cob?

**GREMLINS** used to be helpful. They can make tools, guide the hands of workers, and help with complicated problems. It was the gremlins who whispered the secrets of science and invention to the first alchemists and necromancers. Unfortunately, humans made the mistake of failing to respect the gremlins, and gave them no credit for their magic, so the gremlins got angry. Now they take great pleasure in making sure the Gremlin Factor is built into every machine, especially computers. The Gremlin Factor can best be explained by the rule that "if it can possibly go wrong, it certainly will." Baby gremlins practise their craft by making the wheels stop turning on toys and the chains fall off of bicycles. They are the ones who jam the wheels of your skateboard and dump you in the ditch, they are the ones who make the TV go crazy right at the best part of the program. Sometimes gremlins can be appeased by making sure there is always cream, cheese, and fruit available to them. Often they will take the food and still put the Gremlin Factor into clocks, radios, even telephones. Gremlins have promised that if we stop ignoring them and stop cutting down our forests, filthying our waters, and tunnelling through the earth, they will stop bothering us. So, it's up to us. . . .

184

**GREOGAGHS** are Old Country goolyguys, easily burned by metal. When humans decided to become technological and turn more and more to machines and inventions and away from nature and magic, the greogaghs and goolyguys had to turn away from them. Greogaghs are loyal, friendly souls who used to safeguard the gardens and orchards and do lots of weeding and watering in return for cheese. They also love bread. And cake. And butter. And yogurt. And they LOVE fruit salad.

**KELPIES** are water horses of the rivers who can show themselves as either horses or humans. Usually kelpies are very bad-tempered. If a person is foolish enough to jump on the back of a water horse, it will run away and jump into the nearest river. If the foolish rider cannot swim well, that rider is not only in deep water but also in deep trouble. But if the person carries a leather bridle at all times and slips the bridle on the kelpie before jumping on its back, the kelpie has to obey the human instead of running away. However, the person should not keep the kelpie too long or make it work too hard, or the kelpie's friends will come, free the kelpie, and curse the human and all her children.

**KNOCKERS** live in mines and subway tunnels. Miners often hear knocking sounds which warn them that the mine is about to cave in. If you hear knocking in the subway, head for steps and get out of there because the knockers are giving warning. Nobody is sure what knockers look like because they are so seldom seen. Rumour has it they are pale because they never go out in the sun, they have big eyes to see in the dark, and they have very large, knob-knuckled hands.

**KOBOLDS** seem to come only in adult male form. They are little men with very wrinkled faces. Kobolds almost always have red hair and red eyebrows, and red bushy beards and moustaches. A kobold is more than willing to work day and night if a person welcomes him and provides what the kobold needs. A kobold requires food, particularly fresh bread and butter, milk, cheese, and fruit, and is in heaven if there is caramel or butterscotch pudding. Kobolds like soft, warm places to sleep. Sometimes, if you have to get up in the middle of the night to go to the bathroom, you might hear the scurry of a kobold rushing to hide himself from view. If you check the cushions in the house, you might find one that is still warm from where the kobold was sleeping. In return for leftovers, scraps, and a comfortable place to sleep, a kobold will work incredibly hard. Kobolds milk cows, feed hens, clean the burrs from the horse's forelock. They gather kindling, they pick insects off the vegetables in the garden, they remind you when the stove needs wood.

But if someone forgets or refuses to provide for the kobold, he will get angry. Then dishes will fall from shelves, people will trip and fall on the steps, the cat will stop catching mice. Further neglect of the kobold causes him to leave, and then everyone in the family will have to work harder. Kobolds are particularly good at amusing small babies. If you watch a young baby, you might see it looking at something you can't see, smiling happily and even reaching for something you think isn't there. The kobold is playing with that baby, talking and singing to her, playing patty-cake, holding her hand to keep her from feeling lonely.

**LEPRECHAUNS** are the shoemakers of the fairy world. A leprechaun is never seen without at least one shoe in his or her possession; it may be in a hand, in a pocket, in a backpack, or on one foot. Leprechauns wear green clothes and a red cap. They have big silver buckles on their shoes and often wear leather shoemakers' aprons. They seem to hibernate in the wintertime and reappear in the springtime. They know how to get the gold in the pot at the end of the rainbow, they know where treasure is buried, they know how to turn pebbles into gold and jewels. If you can capture a leprechaun and hang on to him or her, you can force the leprechaun to give you a treasure or three wishes as ransom; however, leprechauns are very crafty and it can happen that no sooner do you grab one than he or she blows sneezing powder into your face and by the time you've stopped sneezing the leprechaun is gone. Also, the three wishes may not turn out to be exactly what you had in mind. One young man, for example, asked to be the most popular person in the world, and nearly went out of his mind with the visitors at the door all the time, the phone ringing day and night, and people coming up to talk to him wherever he happened to be. He couldn't have fun at a party because everyone crowded around him, and when he went to a dance he couldn't even get out on the floor to dance because young and old, boy and girl, they gathered around him talking all at the same time. His second wish was that the first wish be undone, and the third wish is still waiting. He is afraid to ask for anything in case it turns out badly, too.

**LESHIES** are forest sprites who try to protect the forests from unrestricted logging which people seem determined to commit. A leshy (or leshie) is small, wizened, and wrinkled, with bluish skin and green hair and eyes. The leshy tries to tempt loggers off the path, into the bush, where they get lost. In the wintertime the leshy removes footsteps in the snow. The leshy will often try to trip you and before you can get back up again, he or she will steal your shoes. One way to trick the leshy is to wear your shoes backwards, so the leshy doesn't know whether you're coming or going. Even so, he or she will follow you until you feel so uncomfortable and so worried you gladly leave the bush.

**MERMAIDS** live in the sea but can make themselves at home on the land, too. They often sit on rocks and comb their long hair, singing songs which human people think are beautiful. Mermaids have silvery bodies, green eyes, and long hair. While they have tails like fish when they are living in the water, when they come to land they can change their fish-tails into legs so they can walk. Mermaids are beautiful, and can sing and dance wonderfully, but they are terrible cooks—all they like to eat is raw fish and seaweed. They make very good friends but always take your own lunch when you go to visit them!

**NEREIDS** and **NYADS** are sea nymphs, the granddaughters of the gods of the sea and Gaea the earth mother. They are like mermaids but they have lovely long legs instead of tails. They are very vain and quite selfish. They do not make good friends.

**NIXIES** are water sprites, who live in streams and pools. Female nixies are very beautiful, with blue eyes, long fair hair, and little turned-up noses. No one is sure what male nixies look like because they are too shy to show themselves to people. Nixies like to sit in the sun and comb their hair and sing with the birds, but if they hear people coming, they jump into the water, so usually all you see are the ripples. However, if you sneak up quietly, barefoot, with a present (like flowers), you might get a glimpse of the nixies.

188

**NYMPHS** are beautiful fairy maidens who live in plants and trees. Dryads live in the forests and trees, nappies live in glens and groves, orryades live in mountains, ravines, and crags. Nymphs seem to do little more than have a good time. They are very shy, perhaps even frightened of humans. They do not wear clothes. They have beautiful singing voices but sometimes they yell and screech to tease people. They often cause trouble because of their mischief and some of them have taken revenge if a favourite tree is cut or a favourite grove destroyed.

The **OLD LADY OF THE ELDER GROVES** lives inside the elderberry trees. Usually seen in the spring when the elderberry is covered with white flowers or in autumn when the berries are ripe, she is a tiny old woman, dressed in a long black gown with a cap and shawl as white and lacey as the elderberry flowers. Elder wood should not be used carelessly: wasting it brings very bad luck. If it must be used for something other than magic wands, then the person must ask Old Lady of the Elder Groves for permission, and must promise, "When I grow into a tree you may have my wood."

**PIXIES** or **PISKIES** or **PISCIES** are smaller than a grown man's hand. But they can change their size when they have to. They have red hair, pug noses, and mocking—even malicious—smiles. (Most people with red hair and squinting green eyes, pug noses and wicked grins, are pixies in disguise; do not offend them!) Both male and female pixies wear short little tunics with raggedy edges. Pixies seem to be dedicated to making sure humans get lost—perhaps they do not appreciate the way people cut down trees and destroy pixie homes. Sometimes you can fool them by wearing your clothes inside out and back-to-front; this may be why young children don't like to wear their clothes "the right way" and often walk around with their gumboots on the "wrong" feet.

**POOKAS** or **POOKIES** or **PUKAS.** Like pixies, these creatures wear green, but the pooka is less mischievous and less angry. The pooka plays a willow flute, helps take care of the garden, and looks after small animals but never domesticated animals. He only likes wild animals and is especially fond of the Vancouver Island marmot, which may be why the marmot has managed to survive in spite of the logging companies. The pooka plays tricks on people: just as you reach for the shovel it falls over, or you step forward to take the rake and it flies up to hit you in the face, or you spill water all over your clothes instead of on the garden. You go to the garden to gather lettuce for a salad and before you get it to the house, you drop it. Sand or grit is found in the gas tanks of chain saws. That's a pooka at work.

**SEA SERPENTS** come in all colours and live in all seas and oceans. They are usually not very pleasant, but occasionally there are rumours of kindly ones. Only the brave and kind ever seem to find nice sea serpents, and most of the stories about them tell of ships wrecked and sailors eaten. So be very careful.

**SILKIES** or **SEALKIES** were originally seals. They are capable of leaving their seal skins behind and walking on the earth as women or men. They often live with or marry humans, and have even been recorded as having children. Silkies are beautiful, with soft, lovely hair. Unfortunately, their children have a tendency toward pointed, carnivore-like teeth, and seem overly fond of the taste of raw fish or fresh blood. There are many stories of silkies falling in love with humans and bringing great fortune with them, but somehow the people always seem to ruin things. For example, silkies insist on their personal autonomy and privacy. Sooner or later the human spies on the silkie and she goes back to the sea, taking the children with her.

**TROLLS** are usually found in caves, caverns, culverts, and ditches, and under bridges. They appear at night, most often in autumn and winter. When a troll comes out, the birds stop singing, the cows stop giving milk, the chickens do not lay eggs, and the garden starts to wilt. Clouds cover the sky when a troll comes out in the daytime, because sunlight turns them to stone. You may have seen stones that have ugly, misshapen faces hidden in them, the faint outline of arms and legs. . . that stone used to be a troll, but the sun came out from behind the clouds and changed him.